HOW TO GAME PEOPLE
WITHOUT EVEN TRYING

Books by Elizabeth Cooke

LIFE SAVORS

EYE OF THE BEHOLDER

A SHADOW ROMANCE

THERE'S A SMALL HOTEL

SECRETS OF A SMALL HOTEL

THE HOTEL *NEXT DOOR*

A TALE OF TWO HOTELS

RENDEZVOUS AT A SMALL HOTEL

HOW TO GAME PEOPLE WITHOUT EVEN TRYING

A Daughter's Legacy

A Novel

To Rod —

ELIZABETH COOKE

Best, Buffy

ARCHWAY
PUBLISHING

Copyright © 2015 Elizabeth Cooke.

All rights reserved. No part of this book may be used or reproduced by any means, graphic, electronic, or mechanical, including photocopying, recording, taping or by any information storage retrieval system without the written permission of the publisher except in the case of brief quotations embodied in critical articles and reviews.

"How To Game People Without Even Trying," is a work of fiction. Names, characters, places and incidents are products of the author's imagination or are used fictitiously. Any resemblance to actual events, locales, or persons, living or dead is entirely coincidental.

Archway Publishing books may be ordered through booksellers or by contacting:

Archway Publishing
1663 Liberty Drive
Bloomington, IN 47403
www.archwaypublishing.com
1 (888) 242-5904

Because of the dynamic nature of the Internet, any web addresses or links contained in this book may have changed since publication and may no longer be valid. The views expressed in this work are solely those of the author and do not necessarily reflect the views of the publisher, and the publisher hereby disclaims any responsibility for them.

Any people depicted in stock imagery provided by Thinkstock are models, and such images are being used for illustrative purposes only. Certain stock imagery © Thinkstock.

ISBN: 978-1-4808-2103-3 (sc)
ISBN: 978-1-4808-2104-0 (hc)
ISBN: 978-1-4808-2105-7 (e)

Library of Congress Control Number: 2015948608

Print information available on the last page.

Archway Publishing rev. date: 08/25/2015

No man can serve two masters: for
either he will hate the one and love the
other, or else he will hold to the one
and despise the other. Ye cannot serve God and mammon.

Matthew 6:24

PREFACE

"How to Game People Without Even Trying" is a fictional story, inspired by real persons and events that transpired in the 1970s, involving the two-week period prior to the death of Saul Mammon. The personality and modus vivendi, in this tale, are genuine depictions of a very real man.

Just who was Saul Mammon?

He was not one-dimensional. He had charm, wit, humor, an engaging smile. He was full of vim and vinegar and an overwhelming vitality. He was also devious, sly, and too brilliant for his own – or anyone else's – good.

Some of the things he said, his manner of speech, are literally quoted verbatim in "How To Game People Without Even Trying" from the lips of the actual person who lived Saul's fictional life. However, there are other expressions of his that help define him.

"Everyone is trying to prove his cock is bigger than the other guy's."
"Sing them a song leading to a wrong conclusion. But be sure to start with a truth. I call this 'the big myth' technique."

"Get the tickets. He who's got them runs the company or organization. Maybe the world! – Money, Stock, Secrets. Bits of information that embarrass."

Saul Mammon knew how to blackmail.
"You have to keep thinking around them all the time. Ever seen a really good fighter? Always moving. Bouncing on the balls of his feet. Staying loose. It's the same in business. Confuse the other guy so he can't get his footing."

He knew how to unbalance the adversary.

Who was Saul Mammon really? An expert at divide and conquer?
A man who could sense a vacuum and fill it with anything he – or the other guy - desired?
A player of sheer unadulterated guts and boldness, coolness under fire, arrogance, audacity, gall, nerve, loaded with chutzpah? A colleague once said of him, "He's the kind of operator who would always make sure he was standing when the smoke cleared."

Saul Mammon was all of the above. He knew how to seduce people. He'd zoom in, help them to their dreams, or make them think so. Yet he lost the wife he loved and destroyed every relationship, except for that with his daughter.

Saul Mammon's business associates, many as venal as he, as well as the powers that pertained in Moscow behind the Iron Curtain, during this period, cast a spell of conflict overall. His involvement with the CIA only compounded the sense of secrecy surrounding him. His violent death concluded with major questions as to the circumstances of his murder.

Saul's demise was the biggest mystery of his life, of all the mysteries. It fomented a mammoth cover-up, and still, rumors swirl as to his relationship with a powerful, Washington, D.C. columnist for whom he worked, early in the game; as to his association with the <u>Daily Worker</u> and the U.S. Communist Party; as to a Congressional Hearing on a Russian art theft, where he admitted to working with the KGB; even a suggestion of a complicit association with the assassination of Bobby Kennedy.

A friend to Greek billionaires. A friend to Soviet figures on the highest levels of government. A friend to Israel. A friend to the owner of a conglomerate of high priced European hotels. A friend to a renowned New York City lawyer, to bank presidents, to movie moguls. A friend to Senators in Washington, D. C. and even to Presidents of the United States.

However, friends for only a while. In every case, there came a passionate falling out that ended in bitterness, hatred, always dangerous, and finally, lethal.

But oh, how Saul Mammon loved the game. It was the zest, the almost erotic motivation of his life. And no one could game people better. It came so naturally to him, Saul Mammon didn't even have to try, until, in the end, he over-reached. He gamed too far.

The events in "How To Game People Without Even Trying" are a fictionalized account of the truth. The facts, venues, political climate are accurate and without question. Saul Mammon is the avatar of a very real man.

I know. I was married to him.

PROLOGUE

MEDFORD TEXAS, WINTER, 1929

'N.Y. BOY WITH 189 IQ – SAME AS EINSTEIN!' This was the headline in <u>The Medford Evening Star</u> on February 11th, 1929, accompanied by a picture of Saul Mammon's frightened 10-year-old face, with calipers framing his temples.

Who was Saul Mammon, later Master of the Game? The boy learned early how to touch and twist the psyche, heart, and ambition of Victim, Friend, Foe, Lover.

Saul Josiah Mamminiski was born in Brooklyn, N.Y. in 1919. His father died when little Solly was six years old, an only, lonely child. Saul's widowed, Russian-born mother took the boy to Medford, Texas, to her sister's, the winter he was 10, because his mastoids had flared up so badly in the damp and freezing Brooklyn cold, she thought Texas a better place to recover.

His mother had promised the little boy that the doctor's probings would not hurt, but they always proved to be excruciating, and the peroxide afterwards stung him. He never trusted his mother after her false promises. By the time they reached Medford, Solly had lost all hearing in his left ear. It was like stone. In that benighted town,

Saul attended public elementary school. He found himself a pariah. The other children laughed at his Brooklyn accent, but the teachers considered him a rare bird. His brilliance was so distinctive, they measured his talents with IQ tests and calipers, and publicized his uniqueness in the Medford Evening Star.

When Solly returned to Brooklyn, the ostracism was even worse. With a large, white bandage over his left ear, snaking down the Brooklyn street, a plump boy, revolving as if on uneven wheels, (his left leg was shorter than the right,) he seemed a freak to the other youngsters.

He began to carry books from the public library up by Grand Army Plaza, back to his room, which grew to resemble a dusky lair. Solly read avidly, over and over again, the biographies of great men of power who made kings do their bidding. Disraeli, Napoleon, Theodore Roosevelt, Rasputin. He had a favorite. It became his handbook. The workings of the byzantine mind of The Prince by Machiavelli, he committed to memory. "He should be compassionate, guileless. If he needs to be the opposite, he knows how." Saul took 'The Prince's' words to heart.

He would lie on his bed reading, chewing the contents of little, yellow boxes of Chiclets, which his guilt-ridden mother provided, along with the newspapers of all of New York's five boroughs. His room was cluttered, the bed rumpled, piled high, while below on the street, boys played 'Kick the Can' beneath his window.

One evening, Solly stood at that window looking down on the despised street game. He was wrapped in a towel. The doctor had just left from his weekly visit, after painfully poking peroxide into the deep mastoid scar at the base of Solly's left ear.

One of the street boys looked up and saw him in the window. "Hey, Solly," he called.

The other boys paused in their game. They looked up too, and then began together in singsong.

"Hey, Solly,
Come out to play. Sorry, Solly,
We forgot your ear muff."

There were hoots and catcalls from the street. Contorted with rage, Solly turned from the window. The boys continued their game as darkness fell. It got rough enough on the dark street for them to pause, rubbing kicked shins. One boy, kneeling, glanced up again at the window. He clapped hand to mouth and pointed in its direction.

There, silhouetted against the lamplight, was the body of Solly suspended by a rope. Even the outline of his 'ear muff' was there. It seemed he had hanged himself. The street boys let out a collective screech and fled, leaving the grisly effigy in the window, swaying in the evening breeze. Inside his bedroom, Solly sat on the floor in the corner, his round body shaking with laughter. The hanging figure in the window was made of two pillows, a belt, an old bandage for the 'ear muff,' all suspended from a coat hanger by doctor's gauze.

Saul Mamminski had confounded those first enemies. Young Solly had figured out how to bell the cat and warn the birds he was dangerous. It was only the start of a rollicking modus vivendi that continued for the next 50 years. And it all came naturally to Saul, the one-up-man-ship, the machinations he had learned so well from Machiavelli. He knew how to game people. There was no one more adept than Saul Mammon, none more sly, more devious, and most often, the winner.

Well, not always. Not in the end.

Chapter One

Saul Mammon boarded the Concorde this frosty December morning – December 15th, 1979, to be exact - as if he owned it. Sara, in her seat by the window, recognized her father's charm. It was formidable, as she watched him swing down the aisle toward her in his vicuna coat and black fur Russian hat. He greeted the crew – even the Captain – with easy familiarity in a bastard French that put them all in grand good humor for the brief flight of the proudest plane to fly the Atlantic.

Saul Mammon. Her father. Not handsome was he, with the black-rimmed glasses, the stocky figure, but he was compelling. Everyone watched him, heads turned as he passed down the aisle to find his seat beside his daughter.

Saul Mammon had a way of beating time by flying backwards, logging hundreds of thousands of air miles every year. Today, for the first time, she was on his magic carpet. He had invited her to Paris for Christmas and beyond, three months, in fact, to be part of his whirlwind world.

"Hi, kid. You made it," he said as he stood in the aisle beside her.

Sara grinned up at him with delight from beneath the new, bright green cap set back above short, dark bangs. He removed his coat and hat, handing them to a stewardess, and plunged into the seat next to her.

"Welcome aboard, Sara." he said, as the Concorde, after a bone-rattling vibration on takeoff, lifted its haughty nose to the skies and flew off above the clouds, smooth as silk.

Saul Mammon was at home on the Concorde. He delved into his briefcase, studied his papers, spoke softly into his tape machine. To Sara, the morning droned on, time eating itself up, each hour swallowing the next. She stole sly glances at him and dreamed wistfully of the days to come. For the first time, she might be his hostess. She would charm his friends with her wit …unless Renata, the German girlfriend he had picked up on a trip to Berlin last year, was still with him. She was afraid to ask.

How she wished to dazzle Paris, on her father's arm, the two together. Oh, sure, she thought, suddenly coming down earth, smoothing the skirt of her black suit. Good old Sara had yet to dazzle anyone.

Finally, he took off his glasses and leaned his head back.

"What were you doing?" she asked softly.

"Confounding enemies," he said, replacing his glasses, as he turned to her. Enemies, she thought. Her mother always claimed Saul Mammon had a lot of them. Sara wanted to take his hand and hold it quietly. She did not dare. Still, she was just happy to be close to him.

Feeling a little foolish, she ventured the words, "How do you do that, Daddy?"

"Do what?"

"Confound your enemies?" Her body turned to face him.

"Me? Enemies? Did I say that?" His dark eyes twinkled behind the heavy-rimmed glasses of which she wore a smaller version, an almost identical pair.

"I know you have enemies, to be so strong in business," she fumbled, "Tell me how you confound them."

"Why?"

"I want to do it too."

"You have enemies? Already?" he said in mock horror. "At 23 years old?"

"No."

"Then who's to confound?" He laughed, slapping his thigh.

"I want to be like you."

He looked at her hard. "You already are."

"I want to creep inside you and get behind your eyes, peer out through them."

"You might be frightened by the view."

"Oh, no. Not me," she said, bold beyond her feelings.

"Maybe from my perch there's nothing to see."

"Or everything."

"I don't know which is worse," he said soberly.

Sara felt safe on the Concorde, slipping through the atmosphere without a ripple, suspended between two worlds, two lives: America and her pursuit of art in New York City, in her studio apartment in the Village, with a loving mother, Anna, not far away in an apartment on Riverside Drive, and in contrast, this plane, this world, the vastly sophisticated continent of Europe over which her father seemed to preside.

Sara's eyes hadn't left her father's face. She knew it embarrassed him but could not help it. She was trying to discover who he was. Saul Mammon, née Mamminski. Who was he really? She had to know. She determined to know. Perhaps, if she discovered his truths, she might discover herself. This trip was a mission.

Why was he here on the Concorde rather than someplace else? Why was he from Brooklyn? How did he get to play on the world stage? And family? Even her mother, Anna, never knew why his face would close down, leaving her in the dark. She had told Sara this often enough.

A glass and chrome cart slid down the aisle, breaking Sara's spell of scrutiny. It was pushed by two French stewardesses. From side to side they dispensed their wares and their smiles bowing like a pair of orchestrated birds, tall on their high heels, and sexy in their well-tailored uniforms. Although one was blond and the other a redhead, they were interchangeable.

"A cocktail, Monsieur Mammon?" asked the redhead. "Some wine?"

He shifted his seat to an upright position. A suggestive smile curled his face. "What're you selling? What you got special today?"

The girl flushed. He ordered a vodka martini, for Sara, a glass of *Chardonnay*. The redhead adjusted the tray tables, leaning seductively close to Saul Mammon in his aisle seat, her breast touching his arm. She placed the drinks, with paper napkins, silver foil packets of nuts and a dish of four giant, stuffed green olives, their pimentos garish, on his table. He picked one up licked it, watching as the stewardesses moved on, then bit it in half.

"Come on, Daddy. It's all too vague. Give me an example."

"Of what?" he said mischievously.

"Of confounding. Of the way you do business."

He proceeded to munch nuts rapaciously, the jaws moving in grinding bites. Then he hunched forward in his plaid jacket, showing a flash of red suspenders.

"Okay. A few years ago, a guy from Quebec made a run on the stock of MGM. He turned out to be a proxy raider, you know, a guy who tries to take over a company by buying up all the stock he can, to get the majority shares. He'd heard there was oil under the old MGM lot. Manny Kiser, the hot-shot lawyer… you know, Manny and his wife, Gladyce…?"

Sara nodded. Manny Kiser had always made her nervous, but then a lot of people did. She was fully aware how easily she could be rattled.

"Manny hired me to defend MGM, to rally the stockholders, appeal to good old U.S. loyalty against the Canadian son of a bitch. They paid me well. What Manny and MGM didn't know was the guy from Quebec was in my apartment nightly. He paid royally for privileged information and I got his strategy. MGM never knew. Manny never knew. But the studio came out whole."

"Isn't that like working two sides of the street?" Sara was shocked.

"So what? Nobody got hurt, except the Canadian and he deserved it. El Grabbo."

"A secret double agent, you were."

"Nothing so glamorous. Maybe a pirate."

"What if you lose?" she asked softly.

"You bounce," was the immediate reply.

"What a picture. A bouncing pirate, born in Brooklyn," Sara said, laughing, but underneath she felt deeply troubled.

Her father's face suddenly turned serious. "Put yourself where people need you, in the center. Don't be a nebbish, the person at the party whose name nobody can remember." There was a pause. "Look. You're a fine girl. Stay that way. Dress well, expensive. Soak up things like a sponge. If you throw a bash, don't just give it to have a good time. Put people together like equations that add up to your own answer. And listen, listen, listen. The rest is garbage. Am I getting through to you?'

The stewardesses glided back with another loaded cart, this time slices of smoky *paté* with cornichons, baskets of French bread, *châteaux*-grown bottles of wine. The butter was cold and sweet. Her father dipped into the food with enthusiasm. The two ate in silence.

After lunch, Sara watched him sink back and sleep, his face in repose, a mask behind the black-rimmed glasses, stripped of the keenness of eye, the mouth still, the crease of dimple gone. He looked passionless, like an unbeautiful Buddha in a costly plaid jacket. How she wanted to trace that face.

She turned to the clarity of the sky through the small window of the Concorde. How long had it been since she'd seen him? Seven months? Eight? Last June, she calculated and only for dinner while he was in New York at The Pierre Hotel where he kept a suite.

How little she knew him. He was the man who sent the

money – lots of it – who from time to time invited her to dinner. More often than not, the dinner appointments were broken at the last minute for business reasons, but when they did take place, they were evenings of the best table and wine, at Trader Vic's or the Pierre Grill, where he always ordered something out of season, fresh tuna flown from Japan or figs from Morocco. There would be soft music, obsequious headwaiters, and usually an exhortation for her to get new clothes, a stylish haircut, something.

Who was this man, who had supplied a huge house in Westhampton Beach in summer, when she was a little girl? Ah, those summers. There was a special swing for her in the rose garden and a small wading pool. Later, after the divorce, that beautiful summer place would be filled with consorts in various shapes and sizes when Sara visited.

Still, she had never learned to get over the thrill of anticipation in being under his wing, and again, as always, Sara unreasonably expected her golden father to belong to her and her alone. Even while temporizing, telling herself to calm down, she could not help but soar as high and shining as the craft in the sky. Underneath it all, Sara knew Saul Mammon could never belong to anyone.

She had packed for the trip to Paris with care; a long, navy silk gown to wear in the evenings, a couple of crisp suits for daytime Paris and the art museums, a black wool dress that she fancied made her dark looks those of a gamine.

Sara knew how much her father cared for presentation, for the way things looked, especially people. She always felt he found her lacking, somewhere clumsy, not smoothly put together like her mother. When she was about eight, he bought her an English riding habit and smart, short boots and made her wear this costume, screaming, atop an enormous horse, mortally afraid. And the skating skirt. The high-laced white leather skates. And ankles that wobbled like Jell-o. Talk about humiliation. The other girls, in their plain snowsuits and black skates, how they had laughed.

But that was long ago, and now there was Paris and she was

all grown up. With three months leave of absence from her job at Graphic Arts, Inc., off Seventh Avenue, she felt she'd been given an extraordinary gift: a time to live once again, as she had so briefly as a child, beneath her father's roof and in his aura; a time to show him how she could love him. Once her mother had said rather bitterly to her, "Love people, Sara. Love your father. He needs it."

As they were about to land at Charles de Gaulle Airport, he wakened. He turned to her with his engaging smile, and reached a forefinger to the dimple in her cheek, so like his own. His touch felt like a feather brushing her skin.

"You'll be my eternity. Did you know that? Just you, kid. We're so alike. You'll keep me alive forever. Immortal."

A look so intense passed between the two, Sara was unable to swallow. She made as if to caress the long scar behind his deaf left ear, a sensual gesture, but something snapped between them and he turned from her awkwardly.

Chapter Two

There was a storm over the city of Paris that afternoon of December 15th. The Parisians hid in doorways, heads bowed to the blackened skies and the vaguely flashing air. Even the Concorde bumped on landing.

Saul Mammon and Sara were met by Claus, the chauffeur, a tough, middle-aged German, and whisked by limousine through the boulevards to number 17, avenue Foch in the elegant, quiet quartier, the 16th Arrondissement near the Étoile. The clouds seemed to hover over the building with menace.

They entered through the outer courtyard and stepped into the tiny cage-like *ascenseur*. Claus struggled with the luggage up the adjacent stairs to the enormous apartment on the *troisième étage* that was Saul Mammon's Paris home.

The two entered through a bolted, heavy oak door, passed through the circular foyer with a mural of an English garden, and down the long, red-carpeted hall to the bedrooms. Claus brought up the rear. No one spoke.

Halfway down the corridor, they stopped at the room that was to be Sara's while she was with her father in Paris, a beautiful bedroom, all decorated in beige and cream silk. Moving off down the hall, with a tilt of his head, her father said, "I'm down at the end."

Claus left her bags at the door. She picked up her suitcase and placed it on the foot of the bed. Too keyed up to unpack, she went to the double closet, and taking off her suit, put on a long white robe, left there for guests, and walked slowly down the hall to her father's bedroom.

It was like entering a womb, a strange, dark chamber. Here, he must feel safe, Sara guessed, because there were no locks on his bedroom door. The enormous room was completely covered in deep-pile carpet, a chocolate color, even on the walls and ceiling. It was filled with furniture made in Switzerland, covered in cloth of a scorched copper color, with gleaming brass legs. On the desk between two French doors over the courtyard was an eagle-shaped lamp. It gave off subdued light through the twin holes of empty eye sockets. The lamp was made of gold.

Her father lay fully clothed, his shoes off, on the giant bed. It was wrapped in velvet and centered the room on a raised stand. He seemed pensive.

Sara walked tentatively to the French doors and looked out through *voile* curtains to the threatening sky.

"Where's Renata?" she asked in her most casual voice, hoping he would answer 'Oh, she's long gone.'

"Shopping. Where else?"

Sara's heart twisted in her chest. The woman was still in his life. She went and sat on the opposite side of the bed as if to comfort him for his wayward mistress. It was more to comfort herself.

"Why her, Daddy?"

"Why who?"

"Why Renata?'

"Why not Renanta?"

"She's only a few years older than me," Sara mumbled. "She's German. She's a professional."

"You're going to be my hostess while you're here, right? You talk that way about a guest?" he said, bristling.

"Guest? Renata's not a guest. She's more like a piranha," she burst out. She couldn't help it. "You're her victim."

"When have I ever been a victim?" he said, looking straight ahead. Then, turning to her as she rose from the bed, "You go around with the snappy tongue and the mean remarks, you'll blow everything," he continued. " Listen. She's not much, but she pleases me. Don't knock it. At least it's something for the old man, no?"

"Are you going to marry her?" Sara said over her shoulder, her hand on the doorknob.

He did not respond.

"Daddy…"

He came to stand beside her at the door in his socks, walking unevenly. She suddenly realized he was not much taller than she.

"Don't worry about me. Worry about you." He ducked his head, fingering his left ear. "I swear I was born with a permanent bandage, always itches," he mumbled.

"Daddy…"

"Hey, kid. Don't be too much like me. You are, you know." His guard was down.

""I love you, Daddy."

"You'll find someone of your own, Sara."

"I need to know you. I want to be part of your world here."

"I'm not sure you should."

"Of course I should," Sara cried. "I want to sit at the head of your table, go to your office, see how you operate. I want to understand you." It was a plea.

"Why?"

"Because there's no one like you." She stood there in the dim light, eyes glistening with tears.

Saul Mammon looked taken aback. "Oh, please, Sara. Cool it," he said gruffly. "Besides, you might be shocked. I told you, you could be frightened by the view." He turned from her quickly and walked unevenly toward the bed.

"I won't have supper tonight," she said, her voice barely audible. She left him there, her spirit so troubled, it seemed to push her down the hall.

Sara crossed to her spacious beige and white room and lay down on the bed with the disturbing realization that her father just could not understand that if she found the key to him, she might find the key to herself.

Still, on that bed at number 17, avenue Foch, she luxuriated in the capsule her father had established in the center of Paris. Her mind was filled with echoes of things he had told her, of the little boy mischief of the past. She could not help but recall anecdotes she had heard from his Russian-born mother, her own grandmother, long since dead. "When your papa was a little boy about your age, he used to sit in the bathtub and make piles of the globs of GOLD SHAMPOO. They looked like little coins and he'd squirt them in the air through his fingers." GOLD SHAMPOO. Like little coins of gold, Sara thought. Saul Mammon was still squirting them through his fingers just to watch them spin.

Sara's grandfather had been a diamond merchant. The family wasn't exactly poor until Mr. Mamminski died of a heart attack in the street in front of their apartment building when returning home from the diamond district in mid-Manhattan late one winter evening. He was not an old man, leaving only frugal holdings to his family from which the rent, necessities, and little else was maintained.

It was quite a leap young Saul had taken, from the streets of Brooklyn; now, the plush apartment in Paris, a yacht called 'The Ottelia' in the South of France, a chauffeur, services of all kinds, travel around the world, most recently, frequent trips to Moscow. Behind the Iron Curtain!

And always a mistress. They never lasted too long. Renata?

She realized that it was on the yacht the previous August that she had first encountered Renata, with her frizzy carrot-colored hair, so tall and thin she looked like a string bean about to snap. What did he see in her?

The thought of that woman made her restless. The sheets on the wide bed were no longer smooth. The pile of unopened fashion magazines that had been beside her were strewn from one end of the silk coverlet to the other.

Hungry, she got up, slipped on the white robe and silently padded up the hall in what she presumed to be the direction of the kitchen. Off the round foyer, she found the pantry. It was dark. She did not turn on the lights. From the rear servants' quarters, she could hear Claus' deep voice speaking German, plus a dim female response. Was he entertaining? Or was Renata back there giving orders for another day?

Sara had decided by 10 years old, after her father's divorce from her mother, Anna, his multiple liaisons must be borne if she was to see him at all. She would just have to bear the motley parade. In the old days, on visiting him on weekends at the house in Westhampton, the female 'guests' came and went in a bewildering stream amid silver boxes from Bergdorf Goodman, golden boxes from Reveillon Furs, pale blue boxes from Tiffany. It had been exhausting for her at such a tender age, the variety of objects and clothes and special appetites – chocolates, cheeses, diamonds, furs, and the round tins of Iranian sturgeon roe. To count these things was as senseless as counting the women themselves. Sara learned this early when she also acquired a singular taste for caviar.

Now at least she could travel with her father as an adult, but the price, apparently, was the presence of Renata. Here in Paris there was no place to hide from her.

Sara reached into an enormous stainless-steel refrigerator near the pantry door, behind the cold soups and champagne bottles for the fresh tin of fish eggs she know would be there in whatever house he lived. In a drawer, she found a silver spoon with a small bowl and long handle. It felt familiar. In the dim light from the foyer, she made out the initials 'SM' inscribed at the base (one of her hot-cereal baby spoons). She dipped into the precious roe. It was gray and glistening and popping on the tongue, evoking a taste of the sea off Long Island where the tow was so great, she was never allowed in far enough. How she had loved the too short summers she'd spent there as a young girl in her father's house near the ocean.

With each pop of a gray egg, she had the taste-memory; the summer world was recreated in her mouth; the rambling old seaside house and her father's voice through its shadows.

When she was in her early teens, she remembered him saying, "Oh God, Sara. Stop galumphing. You sound like an elephant," which hurt her because she saw herself as a graceful September Morn-type, slender and dainty, perched on a rock in the forest. But her father burst that bubble.

Another egg. Another pop. Another sense memory. "Just girls together," one summer would-be stepmother had squealed on a summer day on one of Daddy's boats. Sara remembered digging a small toenail in rage into the expensive lacquering on the wood railing of the twin-engine Hammond, chipping it. That same hot afternoon, her father dispensed drinks from a portable cooler on the deck. She jumped up and down with great thirst. For what, she wondered now. She had screamed "Me. Me. Me." Her father, in one swift gesture, sprayed a bottle of Coca Cola in her face. She stood trembling, strangely elated, as if she'd been suddenly anointed by a wrathful God. They glared at each other, father and daughter, frozen, two pairs of similar mahogany eyes, boring into the other.

During the subsequent pouting session that August afternoon, her father explained to Sara that maybe his lady friend was just a little bit jealous. "Remember. You were here first," he said. "Always will be." She had held the thought to her adolescent chest as if it were part of her skin.

Standing there in the dimness of the pantry of number 17, avenue Foch, Sara closed the shiny, cold tin of caviar, capping the flood of past days that had engulfed her. There was a deep hole in the contents of the can. She returned it to the refrigerator and started to walk toward the foyer, awakening from the ritualistic hypnosis the caviar orgy had produced. A loud, vulgar woman's laugh in high-pitched squeal echoed from the rear rooms. Renata? It sounded like her. What was she still doing back there? She was the personification of all summer-would-be-stepmothers who had fussed over Sara with presents and false laughter and pretend friendship.

Sara had the awful feeling this 29 year old girl from Frankfurt might just be able to bell the elusive cat that was Saul Mammon, permanently and forever.

December 16th, 1979

Chapter Three

The morning was serene after the storm of yesterday. Sara and her father were driven by Claus through winter streets to Saul Mammon's grand offices on avenue Montaigne. It was impressive, his suite of rooms, with geometric-printed carpets and a small, discreet MONETARY TECHNICIANS, Cable address: MONTEC, embossed in gold on the automatic glass entrance doors.

She sat with him in his inner sanctum with the large *Louis Quinze* desk, swept clean, except for the telephone console. The modern instrument looked obscene on the antique treasure. He sat behind the desk, feet propped up on the polished wood, the heel on his left elevator shoe prominent, and talked at length on the phone -- to Amsterdam and Rome and Washington. His right hand, in constant motion, twirled the globe next to the desk with a proprietary air.

"Manny Kiser should be coming in from New York later this morning," he said, glancing at this watch. "You remember him."

Sara flinched.

"Aw, come on," her father said. "Don't be like that. He's a bright man, Manny is, and I need him. He's putting together some deals for me with American companies, deals for me to take to Moscow. Hey, kid. Anyone who wants to do business East and West has got to come to me." He grinned at his daughter between calls.

This was said baldly, as Sara wandered the room, touching the silk curtain fringe, the black lacquer coffee table, the globe as it revolved under her father's hand. She felt the need to prove these things were real. She was pleased that he allowed her this intimacy, that he had wanted her to see him in his lair.

The multiple-lined phone lighted up as another call came in, this time from Moscow. Suddenly, she began to feel intrusive, in the way, ignored by her father. She walked uncertainly outside to the reception room. There, the formal tri-lingual secretary was speaking in French with a young man in a raincoat. He was tall and had bright, intelligent eyes and unruly hair. He exuded an inquisitive vitality that made her pause.

The man stopped in mid-sentence when he saw Sara. He was visually inspecting her, the dark eyes appraising her, her long legs, and tentative expression, as she stood there in the doorway to her father's office, shutting the door behind her. She was struck by his height, his seeming ease and confidence, the determined chin. It was difficult for her to bear his scrutiny. She felt like her father must, under her own gaze, made uncomfortable by the intensity. It seemed he was trying to memorize her physically, the lines of her body, the arc of arm and hand as his eyes ran up and down her body.

"Yes, Mademoiselle Mammon?" said the receptionist deferentially. She wore her blonde hair in a sleek bun.

Sara smiled a fleeting smile at the woman. "Didn't want to interrupt," she said hesitantly. "My father's on the phone." She felt the color rise in her cheeks.

"You're his daughter?" The man sounded surprised.

"Yes." Why did he make her feel so self-conscious?

"Permit me to introduce myself – Denys Déols," he said, his English perfect but softly tinged with French. He stepped toward her and extended his hand.

"Monsieur Déols." The receptionist had half-risen in protest.

"No problem, Germaine." He swept Sara away to a leather sofa against the wall with a hand under her elbow. She felt the size of his hand on her arm, the length of his fingers.

"I write for <u>Le Monde.</u> You must know of <u>Le Monde.</u>" His voice was deep, appealing. "I'm trying to get another interview with your father for the paper."

Denys Déols was doing a series of stories on foreign businessmen in Paris, particularly those with political overtones. On this special beat stood Saul Mammon, American entrepreneur extraordinaire. There was an eventual possibility Déols' series would be picked up by a prestigious American magazine and appear all over the world. He explained this to Sara, words rushing, as he sat her down on the leather cushions. She did not know that this man was an investigative reporter of great repute, a rising star.

Déols stood in front of her. He had stopped talking and was looking down at her again with that heavy gaze. She felt a solidity about him, as if he blocked her path. He was just there. It was a disturbing feeling.

"Are you the only child or are there other little Mammons?"

"Just myself," she mumbled, starting to get up awkwardly.

"You live with your father in Paris?' he said, confronting her face to face.

"Just here for a visit." She was annoyed, particularly when she saw him draw out a small notebook from his raincoat pocket. She walked around him.

"He expects me," she said lamely, nodding toward her father's door, leaving Denys Déols poised with pen in hand.

Her father was still on the phone, but he waved her in with a smile. She closed the door tight against the man outside.

"Well, you know how it is, Cutter," Saul Mammon was saying into the mouthpiece. "Don't worry so much. Novikov's in my pocket."

He hung up the phone. "That was my man at the Embassy."

Sara sat down on a brocade chair.

"Where the hell is Manny?" he said, looking again at his watch.

"Daddy, who's Denys Déols?"

"Is he out there again?"

She nodded.

"He's a journalist. Interviewed me a couple of times. He's something of a socialist, I think." He laughed. "I can tell he hates my lifestyle. And you should have seen him with Renata. He could hardly get the questions out without wincing. Couldn't stand her."

Hooray for Déols, Sara thought. "But I can't see him today," her father continued. "Why do you want to know about Denys Déols?"

She shrugged, wondering herself why she still felt a glow from the encounter with the newspaperman. Her father picked up the frantically buzzing telephone just as Manny Kiser arrived from New York in a flurry of energy. He was a small man, but a dynamism radiated from him, a toughness belying his size. It suggested he was no one to tangle with. The lawyer embraced Sara too fervently, pressing against her in his pinstriped suit. His pointed, avaricious face fringed with curly red-gray hair loomed close to hers as his fingers gripped her arms. She fled to a seat in the corner.

Her father and Manny were putting together a multiple deal with the Russians for American franchises for the Olympics to be held in Moscow next summer. Through his Russian connections, Sara gathered that Saul had gotten the rights for various companies in the States to service the 1980 Games.

Manny was shaking his head in wonder. "It's only the beginning, Saul. You deserve a lot of credit."

"I opened the territory," her father said with glee. "It's as simple as that. It only took 23 trips to that dismal land of the steppes, this year alone," he said grimacing with disgust.

"At least you got Michelson Frères, here in Paris to back you financially, to protect you," the dapper lawyer said with pride. "They underwrote the whole Olympic gold coin deal, God bless 'em.

They've even started to mint them…already! I got you the best, Saul. Michelson Frères! They're a powerhouse in Europe, the leading asset management firm on the whole continent. But Saul – all those trips to Moscow – the apartment there – those things don't come cheap. You gotta watch it."

"Yeah, " Saul said, leaning forward. "But it's worth it to them. Michelson gets a piece of every one of the deals, for American-made T shirts, caps buttons, all with XXII Olympiad, Moscow, printed in gold. Did you sign up Dutton Rex in Omaha yet for that?"

Manny nodded as he opened up the leather dispatch case at his feet next to his polished shoes.

"Then there's the print work," her father continued, leaning back in the chair, hands behind his head, showing the ever-present red suspenders. "The glossy commemorative programs, the regular programs, posters, tickets. Fellstein in New York is salivating for the business."

"Got it right here," said Manny, brandishing a sheaf of legal papers.

"And food, hot dogs, sodas, beer. The guys in the U.S. who cater the ballparks are hot for concessions."

Manny waved another set of papers. "Here," he said, handing over the full set to Saul. "Signed. Sealed. Now delivered."

"I really have something to take with me next trip, all to be paid for in Russian gold." Saul Mammon's eyes glistened.

"No rubles, please." The two men laughed conspiratorially.

"The money will come in through Michelson Frères."

"Through Michelson." Manny parroted.

"I cut these deals," her father said proudly. He was leafing through the various documents.

"Yeah, but how straight," Manny said under his breath.

"Maybe I'll just up them a little…"

Sara sat still, holding her breath.

"Look. It was a hard sell. Everyone was after the Olympic

franchises for this side of the Curtain. Everyone," her father said, glaring at Manny.

"Yeah, yeah, Saul. You don't have to remind me. Even the British. Herman Tyson, chairman of Petroleum Products, Inc. No wonder he's not speaking to you any more. You screwed him out of any part of the Games." Manny's voice oozed satisfaction. He lit a cigarette and sat back inhaling deeply. "Russian gold." Then he sat forward in his chair. "But you better be careful, Saul."

"I deserve a little bonus, don't you think? They won't know it in Moscow."

"Wanna bet? As your lawyer, I would seriously advise you NOT to cheat the Russians. They don't like it."

"And I don't like that word cheat." Her father's voice was harsh. No one moved.

"It's not any old game you're playing here, Saul." Manny said "For you to outwit them, you like the word better?" He puffed his cigarette, regarding her father with cold eyes. "It's damn dangerous."

"Dangerous. Huh. The minute you're born, you're programmed on 'destruct.' We're all damaged. We all contract that particular disease." Her father fingered his left ear. Sara recognized the gesture as a sign of agitation. She had been watching in fascination the by-play between the two men, like a tennis match.

"Don't tell me how to run my business, Manny." Her father stood up behind his desk. He was suddenly very angry. "You fucking lawyers are all alike. You belch out of law school like a bunch of ping-pong balls. Look at you. I didn't buy you. I just rent you, but your own damn ethics and my overpayments make it a lifetime lease."

Sara was staggered by his quick switch from amiability.

"You need me, Saul. I just want you to be careful. Novikov's no dummy. If he thought..." Manny had taken the abuse quietly. He was almost as hard a man as Saul Mammon, but Sara saw the beads of sweat on his skull under the reddish hair.

"Look." Her father sat down and leaned his elbows on the desk.

He pointed a finger at Manny. "I've told you before. You handle the Russians just like you eat an elephant… bite by bite. My first bite," he continued, "the soybean plants, fertilizer, blue jeans… just nibbles." He was holding up one finger. A second finger joined it. "Bite two; The 1700-room hotel off Red Square called The Red Moon, already finished, that can magnificently house the Olympic guests next summer. Who the hell do you think got the permits so it could be built? That's right. Novikov. And who has Novikov under his thumb?" Saul pointed to his own chest.

"And the biggest bite of all?" Saul continued, "The gold medallions, commemorating the Games. Coins in sets for the suckers to keep! And in pure gold!" There was a boyish ring to his laugh as he laughed for a long time.

Chapter Four

The business meeting in Saul's office was far from over. Sara's head was spinning, but she was absorbed, fascinated by the chameleon that was Saul Mammon. His laughter echoed in her ears.

"By the way, Manny, Ephraim Bachman's on his way," Saul announced.

"Bachman again?" Manny rolled his eyes. "He's another one you've got to be careful about, Saul, but with the U.S. people, not the Russians."

Saul Mammon leaned back in his chair again, rocking it, and said in a soft voice, "Hey, Manny. Let me handle Ephraim. I know you think he's soft but don't ever underestimate his wiles." Saul raised an eyebrow." And don't worry about the Russkis," her father went on. "I've got Novikov. The guy's locked in. If his superiors ever knew he was giving me information on the energy needs of the good old Soviet Union…" He paused. "The boys in the U.S. Senate are very grateful for that knowledge."

"Oh." Sara recoiled at her father's cynicism.

He turned to her, his brow furrowed, eyes behind the dark-framed glasses opaque, depthless.

"Don't look so sour, little girl. Believe me, you'll benefit," he said, his voice cold.

Perhaps so, Sara thought, cringing into herself all of a sudden, with a beating heart. Her ominous feelings were cut off when Ephraim Bachman suddenly appeared, ushered in by the good-looking secretary. He had just flown in from Geneva.

Ephraim Bachman was an enormous Israeli citizen, born in Austria, with two metal incisors in the front of his mouth. His home was currently Switzerland. Although Sara had never met him before, she had heard his story from her mother. She liked him on sight. There was kindness in his face, and his eyes sparkled with an innate intelligence.

A late lunch was sent in. This was not the take-out food Sara was used to in her studio, from New York City's delicatessens. It was smoked salmon with pungent capers, cracked pepper and lemons, served with dark buttered bread, but she was too busy watching to eat much. Her father, Ephraim, Manny and she sat at the end of the long conference table in the room adjoining the office. It was warm for December, and the window was open behind them. The curtains made slight, soft noises.

The business conversation had taken a new turn. It was still difficult for her to understand, but she listened hard. She felt like the sponge her father suggested she be, absorbing all that she could. He was discussing a separate situation with Ephraim, different from the Olympic franchise deals. She gathered that the big Israeli ran a holding company in Geneva, set up by Saul Mammon, called GENCOMP.

"Not more contraband electronic microchips from the States!" The lumbering Israeli dropped his fork in disgust. "Ah, no, Saul."

"The Russkis have orgasms over microchips. You know that, Ephraim." Her father ate the smoked salmon and talked with his mouth full. "Those babies 'll be shipped to you from the States to Geneva just like before. Hold them three months. Then ship them back here to me. From there..." He rippled his left hand in mid-air.

"Right into Russian hands." Manny finished for him.

"Look. It's okay for Ephraim's Swiss company to order the microchips from the U.S., and it's okay for a French company like

Monetary Technicians to buy them from Switzerland-namely from GENCOMP," Saul said, turning to the lawyer.

"But it's just not okay for American microchips to go to Russia. It's not only unpatriotic, it's absolutely against the law. It's treasonous," Manny said emphatically.

"It's not illegal from France!" Her father turned to Ephraim, ignoring Manny. "You know the drill, Ephraim."

Ephraim pushed away from the table. "I've lost my appetite." He looked uncomfortable, glancing anxiously at Sara.

Saul Mammon caught the look. "She's all right. She's kin folk." He grinned at his daughter and reached for more salmon.

"But why, Saul? Why?" Ephraim asked. "Microchips," he said with disgust. Saul did not respond.

From the street below, sounds of boys shouting in singsong French drifted into the long room. Sara's father paused, fork loaded. He listened intently to the haunting sound. The expression in his eyes seemed far away.

"When I was very young in Brooklyn, I couldn't play with the boys. Let's just say, in Moscow, I can." He popped the fork into his mouth.

The boy's voices still echoed from the street. Sara had a vision of Solly's effigy swaying in the window with its pathetic earmuff in basrelief, a story he had often told her.

Ephraim shook his head. "The Russians… computer chips. I'm not proud of it, Saul, the 'false flag' operation." His voice was firm.

"You like the money." Her father got to his feet. The meal was terminated. He stood there, looking down at Ephraim. "You missed our earlier discussion on the Olympic franchises and comrade Novikov. For all his largesse, which I alone developed, Novikov expects some sort of payment in return, no?…like microchips, maybe?" He turned on his heel. The two men followed him to his office next door, Manny scurrying behind Saul, Ephraim slower, thoughtful. He gave Sara another anxious smile and touched her shoulder as he passed.

She stayed rooted at the conference table. What were the mysteries of a false flag operation, with Comrade Novikov's microchips, and T-shirts for Russian gold?

Apparently, you couldn't have one deal without the other. She had seen two functionaries of her father's, Manny, the tenacious ferret, Ephraim, the gentle bear. It seemed Saul Mammon had a different instrument in each with which to express two facets of his personality.

Sara had just seen her father's ruthlessness. So Little Solly had never learned to play ball or roller skate, she thought. Her grandma had cautioned Solly, with the diseased ear, such play was too dangerous. Instead, he had learned to top his plaguers with guile and sheer force of will.

At least half an hour had passed before Saul Mammon reappeared in the doorway. He stood there tentatively.

"What are you doing, kid?"

Sara shook her head. She was glad he'd at least realized she was missing. He sat down at the far end of the table and tapped a pencil on its edge, nervous. The two looked at one another for a long moment. It seemed he could read her thoughts.

"Outside... in school and on the streets," Saul said, "they used to call me 'Solly the bull-shitter.'" He gave a self-deprecating laugh.

"Daddy, you don't have to explain yourself to me," she replied, although she was eager for just that.

"Oh, but I do." He tapped the pencil some more. "I didn't care what they called me," he went on after a pause. "Hell, all I wanted was to develop a silver tongue. I used to practice in front of the mirror."

"You did?" She was listening intently.

He got up and went to the window overlooking Avenue Montaigne. His back was to her. "'Mr. Roosevelt, this is the way to do it,' I'd say. 'Go over there and talk to Hirohito. You won't get your balls shot off. Just hold on to them and talk. I'd be glad to come along and take part in the fun.'" He had grown animated, talking through the window, gesticulating with his hands. "And the kid in the mirror would smile back at me as Solly Mamminski made himself up as he went along."

Sara sat there hoping he would not stop.

"Later, that kind of chutzpah paid off. You know what chutzpah is?" he said with a grin.

"I should," she smiled back. "I'm your daughter."

"Well, for me it became a deadly calm in board meetings and willingness to fly thousands of miles at the drop of a dollar bill." He came over and sat in the chair next to her, leaning toward her earnestly. "But from the very beginning, at 17 years old, as a Fuller Brush man, shoving my foot into Brooklyn apartment doors, I moved quickly. By the beginning of the war, I'd opened a crummy office in lower Manhattan with PUBLIC RELATIONS ENTERPRISES stenciled in gold paint on the door." His hand made a sweeping gesture. "Saul Mammon, President. 'Course I was my only employee."

She laughed. "It's a long way from there to here," she said, gesturing around the elegant boardroom.

He gave a pixie grin. "Wasn't easy. First, promotions for products, liquor companies, stores. Then I began to get into local political campaigns, later, to deal with Congressmen and beyond. You know, I found my deaf left ear an asset? It only made the good one more acute, more aware of whispers. I supplied information. Pretty soon, when I'd walk into a room, the place kind of stopped," he went on, his face eager. "They knew who I was and treated me like a somebody. I had it all on the expense account. I used the local bank like a department store." He chuckled. "I paid lawyers and walked out laughing." It seemed to her he began talking as if she wasn't there.

"Get yourself sterilized before you travel second class. Has to be the Concorde. Limo at the airport. Cleared of Customs. Cultivate a free-spending corporate style – but which corporation?" He chuckled again. "There're so many. Safety in numbers."

Sara held her breath. Please don't stop, she thought. Here was the real Saul Mammon.

"And don't let the 'keeping money', ya know, the equity accumulation, arrive after you're gone," he went on. "Always try to really BE a rich man, not just live like one." He grew quiet.

She had not said a word. The afternoon was waning.

"Now I have the best of everything," he said, "in Paris, in London, New York, Geneva, even Moscow. Somebody always knows someone. People come to me and offer shows, dinners, suites, yachts, women... what can I tell you." It was not a question.

"Everybody rides along. Manny, my hatchet man. That way I remain a virgin." Saul chuckled. "And savvy, sentimental Ephraim. Renata for the glamour stuff. She can put on a rag and look great." Sara cringed. "And then there's you, kid," he said softly, turning to her. "You... and your mother, of course, before she decided to get off the gravy train. I never really knew why." His voice was almost inaudible. The light in the long conference room had grown dim.

Sara could not see his face. It was just as well.

Chapter Five

Sara walked slowly down the hall to her bedroom. She felt drained and anxious. That afternoon her father had revealed himself, but he still remained obscure. Solly Mamminski had 'made himself up as he went along.' How in heaven was she to probe that imagination and come to grips with him if he was still doing it?

She closed the bedroom door behind her. On the bed, she dropped her purse and a small package containing new contact lenses picked out by her father on their way home from his office. She unzipped the skirt of her suit. It slipped to the floor encircling her feet. She stepped out of the circle and went to the marble bathroom and turned the shower tap to hot, then took off the rest of her clothes, laying them in a neat pile on a side chair. The black-rimmed glasses she had always worn she put on the sink.

Sara stood in the white room naked. Her legs were long for her height, the thighs rounded, her breasts high. She extended a hand beneath the stream of hot water, then adjusted the tap to a cooler temperature, standing in the deep, old-fashioned tub beneath the running water, relishing the softness of the washcloth, the scented soap. It was a luxurious moment.

She stepped from the tub and with a groping hand found a towel and dried herself slowly. She went to the mirror over the double sink and looked closely at her face. Without glasses, her eyesight was misty. Through the steam, she smiled at herself and Sara-in-the-mirror smiled back, revealing the one dimple in her left cheek that so matched her father's.

But there was a second reflection in the glass. Renata stood in the doorway, one befurred arm leaning high against the bathroom doorjamb, the other akimbo on her hip. She wore a short 'chubby' red fox jacket that matched her hair, and blue jeans taut over her bony behind. She stood there boldly watching the young girl in this private, nude moment.

"What?" Sara exclaimed, wrapping the towel tightly about her body.

"I just wanted to say hello." Renata's accent was guttural.

"How long have you been standing there?"

Renata shrugged. "We is both girls, *nein?*" she said, laughing.

"No. We is not."

Renata dropped her arm, allowing Sara to stride past her and collect the white robe from the closet, hurriedly putting it on over the towel, dropping the terry cloth to the floor from beneath. Renata opened her jacket, revealing a silk blouse, slit to the waist where ropes of gold helped conceal the virtually breastless chest. She sat on the bed and lit a cigarette.

"How long has it been?" Renata said.

"Last year." Sara sat at the dressing table, brushing her hair with angry strokes.

"It was on the yacht – that week in August, *nein?*" Renata pronounced it 'yakt.'

"Yes." Sara remembered it well, Renata scrawny in her bikini. Renata with her oils and the aluminum sun shade beneath her chin and the long, thin arms. She had found her father passionately embracing Renata one afternoon in the boat's salon and those arms had seemed to twine around him like snakes. Sara had been so physically disgusted; she'd cut short her week's visit. She had not seen him since, except for the one evening for dinner in New York last June. That night, he had been alone.

"Hadn't you better be changing for supper?" Sara eyed Renata's stilt-high red leather boots.

"There's time."

"Well, I would like to, if you'll excuse me."

Renata gave her a hard look and gathered up her things, half stubbed out her cigarette in a small ashtray beside, the bed, and sauntered to the door. There, she turned, dramatically tossing her hair.

"Welcome to Paris," she said with a victorious kind of smile.

"Thank you. And Renata, next time, knock," Sara said quietly, and the German woman was gone. Left behind her was the smell of the overpowering perfume '*Valkyrie*,' and a rope of smoke climbing in the air from the ashtray made of jade.

———

It had been a day of lavish eating. Sara's stomach hurt and she had a headache as she sat at the head of the dinner table that evening in the dining room of number 17, avenue Foch. It was an uneasy group, except for Saul Mammon. She watched him at the opposite end of the table relishing the last remnants of chocolate *soufflé*.

Renata, in a brilliant orange caftan sat on his right, a subdued Ephraim on her other side. She was not a pretty woman, but Sara had to agree with her father that Renata wore her extreme clothes with coat-hanger style in her passionate chase after the expensive things in life.

Renata made Sara feel self-conscious in her navy evening dress. Renata's eyes seemed to flicker, 'No style.'

They said other things too, those eyes. The glassy, pale irises had dollar signs deep inside. Renata knew they were there. She had told Sara, having been born shortly after World War II, she'd grown up poor in a Germany devastated by the American bombers. She had never seen a plane, but the destruction and poverty left behind became Renata's rationale for her appetite for goodies. Sara didn't accept this explanation, as it seemed pronounced only to make her feel guilty to be an American.

She found it disgusting the way Renata played up to her father, laughing raucously at his jokes, feeding him daubs of whipped cream from her spoon, licking it after he did.

A good deal of red wine had been consumed during the past hour at the table. Ephraim was waxing nostalgic. "You were different once, Saul – when you first came to Israel in the 50s."

"You're a soft touch, Ephraim."

"We were both full of dreams."

"Who me?" said her father with a grin.

"I'm no longer welcome there, in Israel. You made it impossible for me." Ephraim's voice was low. Sara glanced quickly at her father.

"You got good old Switzerland," Manny said. Suddenly, Sara became aware of his knee pressing her own beneath the table.

"Ah, for my native Austria before the war, before the Germans marched in and the Russians from the other side," Ephraim continued wistfully.

At this, Renata's face turned sour. Her hostility to the Israeli was barely beneath the surface.

"Israel's just Miami Beach with fat ladies spritzing themselves on the sea shore," Saul said, his voice cynical.

"Once you didn't think that. Remember the cave in the hills back of Jerusalem?"

Ephraim leaned forward in his animation, his face suffused with light. The chair creaked under him. "With young people in Israeli khaki singing songs -- Rumanian songs, Moroccan songs – even German songs."

Renata flushed. "Claus," she said, waving her wine glass to be refilled, which he did, even with the carafe right in front of her. She downed the wine in a gulp.

"Anna was with you," Ephraim continued to her father. He turned to Sara.

"Your mother. She was so lovely."

Sara smiled. "She still is," she said, glancing slyly at Renata.

Saul Mammon stopped her pleasure with a look. "Bachman, you're a romantic," he said coldly.

"Ah, but she was lovely, Saul." Then, turning again to Sara, he said, "You are much like her – except dark-haired. But that night – in the cave in Israel," he went on, "you were singing too, Saul. Have you forgotten? Why you even danced the hora. You wanted to de-salt the sea water – make the deserts bloom."

"Yeah," said Manny, "and between the two of you, you practically broke the Bank of Israel."

Ephraim suddenly sounded accusatory. The metal incisors in his mouth gleamed in the candlelight. "You manipulated Israel, Saul… promised so much from the United States you couldn't deliver. You didn't have the right. You wiggled Israel."

"Just like you're wiggling Russia now," Manny said under his breath.

"You know who your worst enemy is?" Ephraim went on.

There was a long pause. Everyone at the table was looking at her father.

"Sitting right here," Saul Mammon said firmly, slapping the arm of his chair.

"I'm my own worst enemy, right? And I should be contrite. It's obscene for a nice Jewish boy from Brooklyn, right?" he gestured around the elegant dining room. "To play at the top, cruise the capitals, drop names that reverberate…"

"Saul," Ephraim interrupted.

"Something within me says I'm not worthy." Her father sounded maudlin.

"I'm sure a psychiatrist…" Ephraim started to say, completely sucked in by Saul's apparent vulnerability.

"Aha! I gotcha. Contrition." Her father threw back his head and laughed.

Ephraim was furious. "Jesus Christ, Saul."

Saul Mammon rose from his chair. "Contrition. That's what you want from me. Well, you're not going to get it. What do you know about being poor and half deaf, with a gimpy leg? They tell you the mastoid operations won't hurt. The hell they don't. Christ, I felt like damaged goods. You don't know what it's like, Ephraim. It makes you different."

Ephraim stood up, knuckles on the table as he leaned across it toward her father. He looked enormous. "Different? Not to play ball or roller-skate? Loaded with self-pity, maybe." With dignity, he tapped the two metal incisors in his mouth. "Rotted out in concentration camp in Poland. No, Saul. No, I don't know what it's like."

The two men glared at one another.

"Hey, fellas," Manny said benignly. He'd been sitting back observing this confrontation with keen interest. "Enough posturing. Are you competing in the suffering department?" Saul and Ephraim sat down again, each in his place. They both looked sheepish. Everyone laughed uneasily.

Feeling the wine, Sara was deeply chagrined by her father's behavior. It made her reckless. Manny had pushed his chair closer to her in the course of the evening. His stiff, graying red hair made a halo-like effect on his head in the candle glow. She could feel his knee underneath the table again, pressing against hers. She decided to yield to it, then, remove her leg, teasing the lawyer until the color of his face almost matched his hair. She was flirting outrageously with him to make her father act the jealous lover.

She poured from the carafe of wine before her, a glass for Manny, one for herself. It spilled on his hand. She took her napkin and caressed the flesh beneath it as she wiped away the red drops, brushing against his arm with her breast as she'd seen the stewardess do with her father. If she was sexually competing for her father's attention, she could not seem to help herself.

"Oh… oh… how stupid of me…" she said coyly.

"It's O.K., kiddie."

"I didn't mean to be so careless," she continued coquettishly, eyes on her father to see his response to her provocative behavior. He was impassive. She touched Manny's sleeve.

"You know, Manny," she said, her voice louder that usual, "You and Daddy are like alter egos."

"*Mein Gott,*" Renata exclaimed contemptuously.

"I try to be useful to your father, " Manny said, flushing further. "Saul relishes every minute -- and dollar – he can escape the IRS. I've a few tricks up my sleeve to keep them off his back – yours, too, if you ever need it." He gave a lascivious chuckle, drinking deep of the wine. "Besides, your back is prettier."

Sara bent to him, eyeing her father. "You grease Daddy's wheels?"

"Or palms," said Ephraim softly.

"Something like that, eh, Saul?" said Manny.

There was a blue tinge of disgust around her father's mouth.

The phone rang in the salon, breaking the spell. Claus answered in the pantry.

Saul was already on his feet and moving toward the adjacent room to take the call.

Renata followed him, her pelvis swaying. Her rib cage with its tiny, button nipples protruding from under the clinging orange *lamé* was so thin it looked as if she could stick her fist up under the bones.

Sara was crestfallen. Any effect on her father of the flirtation with Manny had been broken.

She heard her father's raised voice from the salon. "Shit, Cutter. I thought you didn't believe in calling me at home. Don't ever do it again." Then his voice dropped low and she could hear no words, only the angry rumble of his speech.

Sara became aware that Manny had pushed yet closer. She looked at him. His face was red, one arm around the back of her chair. Suddenly, he took her chin in his free hand and forced a swallowing kiss on her lips.

Ephraim looked shocked. He shook his head from side to side. "Manny... hey..."

"Excuse me," she said nervously. Things had gone too far. She rose from the table, her long navy skirt sweeping the carpet as she ran down the hall to her bedroom and rushed into the adjoining bathroom, closing the door. She leaned back, then moved to the sink, head down. Was she going to be sick?

There was a tap on the door.

"Yes," she said in a small voice as she turned to face the door. She was quivering.

The bathroom door opened. Manny entered and kicked the door shut behind him. He stood there, breathing hard, not saying a word, tie unloosened, dinner jacket unbuttoned. She felt like a trapped animal.

Suddenly he stepped forward. His hands lifted the pleated skirt up and around her waist, revealing her bare legs and the evening slippers on her feet. Her knees bent as she was hoisted onto the sink, Manny pressing between. His trousers had slipped to the tiles, leaving his naked legs covered with prickly red hairs. He was trying to reach her mouth with his own. She could smell his hot winey breath.

"No, Manny... please," she screamed in horror.

"Oh, yes, kiddie, you asked for it."

She felt suffocated, but most of all, she felt her exposure, a moment of terrible openness. Sara managed to put both hands against his shoulders and shove him from her with a mighty thrust. "Stay away from me, Manny," she hissed.

"You're a real little cock teaser, aren't you, Sara," he said, his face furious.

"You disgust me."

"Then what was that crap all about at the dinner table?"

"Daddy," she wailed.

"No need to call him," Manny said, his voice uneven. "Saul wants you for de Bouchère. I thought I'd break in the merchandise."

"My father…"

"He'd never believe it, not in million years. I'd deny it. He'd laugh in your face."

Sara stared at him hard. "You look ridiculous."

That did it. Manny looked down, jerked up his pants and with, "You're a bitch," said so softly over his shoulder she could barely hear him. He left her, escaping as quickly as he had arrived.

She sat there stunned, pulling at her clothes, smoothing down the skirt of the dress she had so carefully chosen. She slid from the sink and pressed against the cold porcelain for many moments. Slowly she went over to the toilet and vomited – salmon and *soufflé* and wine, along with 'false flags' and Russian franchise gold and all of Israel's treasure. They seemed to flush away, all the lavish eating, the quantities of words and deals, her father's 'contrition,' the idea of de Bouchère, and most of all, Manny. Manny went down the drain, leaving her skin clammy, stomach hollow and shaking.

December 17th, 1979

Chapter Six

The pictures in the Jeu de Paume were an exquisite refreshment. Sketchbook under her arm, Sara strolled silently through the small Museum, formerly the ancient tennis court of the Palais des Tuileries, on this wintry afternoon. She was still traumatized by last night's encounter with Manny, not by his actions so much as by her own complicity. She knew she had provoked him, no question.

Ever since her father had shattered her September Morn self-delusion, she had never felt particularly attractive. Yet, last night she had projected something raw to Manny Kiser, something she had not intended. Or, had she? She was not a virgin. There had been the brother of her friend, Suzanne. He was the first. Her second was a man in art school, in fact, the teacher.

The lilting light of the Monets and Cézannes and Seurats helped lift her conscience. Surrounded by the fresh blaze of color from every wall, she felt human again.

She stayed until closing time, taking comfort in the beauty surrounding her until the guard politely ushered her out. She hated to leave. How to return to avenue Foch? How to face Manny again? Or the entrenched Renata?

No one was there when she entered the apartment. Not even her father. How she longed to speak with him, to open up to him, to explain the consequences of her dangerous Manny game. As she turned in the hall to enter her bedroom, she heard a flurry of locks being opened at the front door, bolts slipped, and voices behind. Her father and Renata came into the foyer, she striding ahead of him, taller than he in a suede coat with fringe that swung like a stripper's tassels about her body.

"Ah, there you are," her father called to her down the long hall. "Just in time to drive out to the airport with me. I'm Moscow-bound again." He appeared purposeful, his face as exhilarated as a child's. Renata marched angrily down the hall, swinging past Sara to the master bedroom.

Her father shrugged his shoulders and lifted his hands helplessly at Sara. With a grin, he walked past her and down the hall into the master bedroom at the end, leaving the door ajar. Sara could hear the guttural ripple of Renata's voice, then the rumble of her father's. The words were muted at first, but as Renata's tone escalated, so did Saul Mammon's.

"I say anything I want. Remember on boat – you call me *Chrysou Mou*– 'Golden One' in Greek – when you behave like famous tycoon from Athens? Not so long ago. Saul…y…" Her tone was shrill.

"You're not going to be around here much longer."

"We see about that. You do not get rid of me so easy, Sauly baby."

She could hear her father's derisive laugh.

"I suppose you go back to Anna." Her tone was nasty.

"Leave Anna out of this. I'd sooner have a bad marriage with Anna than be with anyone else – especially you. Little, skinny Yonka Schermeyer – the call girl from Frankfurt who advertised herself as Renata Gulden, as in 'gold.' I must have been crazy."

"Crazy. I take everything you got, new yakt and all."

Her father started to laugh. "You can't even pronounce it." And Sara heard him begin to sing, "For she's a Yonka Doodle Dandy, Yonka Doodle do or die," as he came merrily out of the door and down the hall toward Sara. Renata could be heard cursing in German as she slammed the door.

With a nod to his daughter, he waved for her to join him. After he retrieved a dispatch case from the salon off the foyer, the two descended in the tiny *ascenseur*.

"She's got a burr up her ass," he said and laughed at the thought all the way down to the courtyard.

In the limousine with Claus up front, Sara turned to her father, but he was in the midst of plugging a wire into his tape recorder and had started speaking into it. Names like 'Novikov' and 'Ivanov' and 'Ghisviani' began rattling off his tongue and into the machine. With a sigh, she smoothed the sketchbook on her lap and looked out the window. She wanted to speak to him about Manny, but how? What? Through her frustration, she heard her father's voice saying, "Check the new freezers for the Moscow apartment – air conditioners – Aubusson rugs." She watched the evening boulevards of Paris passing by, lights just beginning to glow, the *cafés* and bistros warm and inviting. They appeared in sharp contrast to her father's matter-of-fact laundry list of luxury. She gathered he had bought an apartment in an old Russian palace and was outfitting it. He continued speaking into the machine for most of the trip to Charles de Gaulle Airport. He clicked it off finally and pulled a sheaf of papers from his dispatch case and began to glance through them, talking all the while.

"When I get back, maybe you and I should go down to Nice to the yacht. It's in dry dock but it's a good idea to see what those jokers are doing to it, not crossing any wires, right, kid?"

It might be a relief to get out of Paris, and away from Renata.

"Maybe I can get Henri de Bouchère to join us." Her father went on, still looking at his papers. "He's got one at the same boat yard. You remember him, Sara. He liked you."

"Well, I didn't like him. He's a toad." Her skin turned cold at the thought of the squat, older man from two years ago, his yacht parked next to her father's at Cap Ferat. She had found de Bouchère repulsive.

"Hey, kid. Watch your tone. You should be so lucky. He owns more hotels in the Mediterranean basin than there are fish in the water. Here, take a look at these," he said, thrusting the stack of papers on Sara's sketchbook. They were the signed American franchise deals. "I'll show the Russians what capitalism is all about."

She passed them back to him.

"And we're going to be paid in gold."

"You know, Daddy, it's amazing for someone who works so closely with Communist Russia, you live like the Tsar," Sara said slowly.

He gave her a quick look. "Now you sound like your mother." He put the papers back in his dispatch case. "You talking about the apartment in Moscow? Hey, I need a place, I'm there so much. Besides, kid," he said with a grin, "they never got over the Tsar." Saul chuckled, shook his head. "How they love power. When I visited Carter last summer to discuss the 1980 Moscow Olympics, I loaded my pockets from the drawers in the hall tables with White House matchbooks as I was leaving. They just loved them in the Kremlin."

He scratched his left ear. "The Russians are easy to read. It's all a matter of hypnotism. One night I was sitting with Yuri Novikov and company in one of those barn-like Moscow restaurants where they put a crock of lousy caviar in the center of the table. I pulled out a coin from Disneyland and started tossing it in the air like this."

He had pulled out a U.S. quarter from his pocket and was tossing it up and down, there in the cushioned back seat of the limousine. It gleamed from the streetlights. Sara's head and eyes followed its movements.

"You should've seen the whole table of Russian heads… up and down… up and down… just… like… yours."

"Daddy…"

He leaned back. "You know, I talk to myself. Oh, yes. I told you that… about Solly-in-the-mirror. But now, in my old age, I have tape machines instead – here in the limo, in every desk, in my dispatch case, even a tiny one in my tie tack. That little bugger is amazing. It can record for hours."

"Why?"

Her father smiled. "You know, I hated Richard Nixon. But, by God, I admired his tapes. He had the guts not to burn them."

"Daddy. I want to talk to you about Manny."

They were already touring down the airport avenue, past warehouses and hangars and parking lots and maintenance buildings.

"What about Manny?" He was closing his dispatch case and brushing his sleeves, eyes outward and expectant.

"He…well he…kind of came on to me." Her face felt hot.

"At dinner last night?" he said, turning his body toward her. "I thought maybe you were coming on to him," he said.

So he had been aware of her flirtatiousness.

"Listen, kid. You can't do that with people like Manny. Save it for de Bouchère. At least he's not married."

Sara felt hopeless, de Bouchère again. A sense of dread overwhelmed her.

The limousine took an alley past the terminal building and wound out onto the airfield. It had begun to rain lightly again. The car pulled up beside the outline of an Aeroflot airliner. Through the drizzle, the huge shape looked sinister, like a great fish under water. Sara could see the ramp to the cabin down on the tarmac. A heavy-set man in uniform descended the steps and came over to the car. He stood at attention beside the door.

"Well, I'm off, kid. Back in a couple of days," her father said turning to her, giving her a quick touch on the cheek. "Listen, I couldn't look at myself shaving if I didn't do my bit for peace."

With that, he was out of the limousine. He shook hands with the Russian. Sara watched him mount the steps to the interior of the plane until he was lost to her. Claus put the car in gear and she was driven away, through planes taxiing, colored lights flashing, through airport sounds muffled by the heavy glass panes of the car, and through a darkness that was descending with the onset of night.

Chapter Seven

Sara arrived back at the avenue Foch apartment just as Renata came into the building. God knows where that woman had been, Sara thought. The two walked across the inner courtyard in silence. There was barely room enough in the *ascenseur* for Renata and herself. She resented having to be so close to her father's mistress, inhaling the distinctive perfume (Frankfurt's best?) She could see the pores of Renata's skin beneath the heavy make-up.

Renata stood there smugly. She entered the oak door of the apartment ahead of Sara. The German woman strode down the hall, disappearing into the master bedroom without a word. Sara went into the green and gold salon off the foyer and sat wearily on an ottoman before her father's easy chair. She laid her sketchbook, which she had been clutching all evening for reassurance, on his seat. Claus poked his head in the room and told her a light supper would be ready within half an hour. She wasn't sure she'd be able to eat.

Suddenly, Renata was in the doorway of the salon, a startling apparition. She had removed her suede outfit and appeared in a skimpy, pailletted dress, with a headband of rhinestones holding back the frizzy hair.

From one finger, she dragged the fox fur jacket after her on the carpet. She puffed away at the ever-present cigarette. Sara studied her.

Her look must have shown contempt, for Renata burst out, "You do not like me, *nein?*"

Sara was unprepared for the remark. "I hardly know you."

"What you not like, *yah?*"

Sara said nothing.

"Jealous?" Renata said with a rapacious smile.

"Hardly." But she knew she was. "How Daddy could ever," she mumbled.

Renata stood in the middle of the room, puffing on her cigarette. "How do you think I meet your father anyway?" she said defiantly. "In convent?"

Sara had to laugh.

"Claus." Renata said triumphantly.

"Claus?"

"*Yah.*" Renata was pacing back and forth. "Claus is good arranger. He's been arranging me for years."

Sara was so disgusted she thought her stomach might erupt again. "So Claus is your pimp," she whispered.

"He's my 'arranger.'" Renata perched on the arm of Saul's chair, again much too close to Sara. It was a proprietary act from which the girl shrank back. "Claus put me at party where your father was guest. Six years ago. Saul and I is off-again, on-again ever since. Now, very much ON," she said, puff, puff. "Your father – very big in Europe, you know, so they say. Not only Europe and Russia," Renata said. "Saul had big deal with the Governor of California, something about oil from Mexico, and big business in Tokyo too – electronics," she said proudly. "He took me there. Awful little yellow men."

"You seem to forget your country was once allied with those awful little yellow men," Sara said coldly.

Renata was taken aback for the first time. "I was not yet born in World War II," she pouted. Then after a moment of sullen silence, she said. "You and Renata, we make friends, Sara. If not just because we are near same age," she said pointedly, "but for Saul. He wants us friends."

"It's not possible."

"You may marry one day over here – Henri de Bouchère."

Not that name again!

"Saul says he has eyes for you." Renata went on, cajoling. "You like to dance, *nein*? Come with me tonight. I go to disco. You don't need man to be with you. There are plenty there. Come. Claus drives us, *nein*? We have good time, exercise, see Paris, hear music, feel the beat."

"YOU feel the beat."

Renata stood up. She shrugged her shoulders. "Well, I try. You are moody, unhappy girl."

"Why were you so mad at Daddy?"

Renata looked blank.

"You know. When you came in together tonight. You didn't go to the airport with him."

"Oh, that." Renata started for the door, dragging her coat after her. There, she turned "You see this fur?" she said, pointing to the poor red garment near her feet. "It's fake," she said furiously. "That's why I fight with Saul. He give me fake." With that, she grabbed the phony fur, and twirled out of the room.

Sara burst out laughing. She couldn't stop. Claus soon appeared in chauffeur's cap. She now saw him as a conspirator. He announced he had to drive *Madame*. Sara's supper was ready and would she like it on a tray, he inquired. It seemed a good idea to try, so she sat in her father's chair and toyed with a cheese omelet, asparagus *vinaigrette*, and a *crème caramel*. It went down all right until she realized she felt like a child in a nursery while the adults were off somewhere at play. Her stomach churned once more. Sara looked bleakly around the over-dressed room, at the Ormolu clock on the mantelpiece with a Vlaminck painting hanging above it (was that fake, too?) She looked at the heavy damask curtains at the two French doors over the courtyard, at the enclosed bar with its crystal decanters. Right now, all she longed for was her one room studio in Greenwich Village in New York, with its enormous back window at the far wall. Her drawing board stood before it.

When she worked there, she could look down on the rear gardens of the scruffy little French and Korean restaurants that face out onto the street below. When the window was open, the air smelled of garlic and ginger and hot oil.

The phone rang. No one was there in the apartment now but she. She picked up the receiver after the fifth ring.

"Yes?" Her voice was desultory.

"Hey, kiddie." It was Manny, oily, suggestive, not a hint of conscience in his tone.

She said nothing.

"That you, kiddie? What're you up to?"

"Goodnight, Manny," she said, making her voice sound as bitter as she could.

"Hey…hey," he said. "No need to be so cold."

"The whole business last night was cold."

He was silent. Then, "Well, you had it coming. Admit it. Didn't you put me on?"

She couldn't answer.

"Well, didn't you? Be honest with yourself."

She still did not respond.

"Where's Saul?" he asked finally.

"In Moscow."

"Oh, that's right."

"I took him to the airport…alone."

It was Manny's turn to be silent. "Did you say anything?" he said at last.

"About what?"

He cleared his throat. "Well…" He cleared his throat again. "Feel like going out on the town? I know a swell *boîte* where they still play good jazz."

"Goodnight, Manny," she said again, and hung up the phone.

She sat there a long time in the darkening room. The thought of Manny quickly distanced itself. He was a mere fleabite. Saul

Mammon was her quest. So far her father's persona provided nothing but turmoil.

Sara turned on the table lamp and picked up her sketchbook. She opened it to a clean white page and with dark charcoal she began to sketch that enigmatic face.

"I'll capture you yet, Daddy. Just wait and see."

December 18th, 1979

Chapter Eight

The next morning, as Sara got out of the tiny elevator on the ground floor of number 17, avenue Foch, Denys Déols stood up. He had been sitting, reading a rumpled newspaper, filling the small lobby settee in the corner of the entry room, his raincoat askew, one ankle crossed over the other knee.

He's so tall, was the first thought that flashed through her mind as he unfolded himself in front of her. She saw in him a raw-boned quality that matched her own. Although he was several feet from her, she sensed his presence like a rock to be gotten over.

"*Bonjour, jolie mademoiselle.*" His grin was infectious.

Jolie! He called her *jolie*. In fact, she felt more *jolie* than usual. In the first place, she was wearing new contact lenses instead of the usual 'owls.' Her father had taken her to Falantrop, Opticians, near the old church, La Madeleine, that late afternoon after their talk together in his office conference room.

This morning was the first time she had applied them, after considerable struggle in the process. She was wearing a dark suit, a white silk shirt, and sheer black stockings.

Had she been expecting Denys Déols? It was almost so. She

nodded at him and tentatively returned his smile. Then moving around him, she headed for the street, a taxi, and the Louvre. She was planning to spend as much time as possible in museums and galleries, starting with the obvious and working her way down to the tiniest atelier she could find. Art was her second obsession, her father of course, the first. Today, on this sunny morning, now unnaturally graceful in the eyes of Denys Déols, she floated out through the courtyard onto the avenue. He followed in close attendance.

"Would you like a coffee?"

"No, thank you."

"Where do you go? May I drop you?"

"I'll pick up a cab," she said with reticence.

"Here's my car." It was an old black Citroën. He held open the door.

Sara hesitated. He made it hard to refuse, as he touched her elbow. She was afraid to look directly into his eyes. She got into the passenger seat without a word and he slammed the door behind her.

"Where to?" he said in his French-tinged English, getting in and revving the motor. The separation – he in the driver's bucket seat –Sara as passenger in hers – seemed formal, a drawing back from some dangerous ground.

"The Louvre, please." She compressed her lips. She could feel him studying her profile for a moment. Then he moved the car forward. They drove to the corner of avenue Foch and around the Étoile in a silence complicated by the fact that from the moment of his hand on her arm, she felt a physical attraction. It startled her. She resisted, but it was there between them in the old car, and it left her dumb and staring out the window.

"Is it rude of me to ask where your mother might be?" he said, finally.

"Yes."

"Yes?"

"It's rude." She had not turned her head. "My parents have been divorced for years." and then she added, "not that it's any of your business."

"*Excusez-moi*," he said politely. Denys Déols was driving swiftly, weaving in and out, honking – everyone honked – although it was against the law. Sara was impassive on the surface. Underneath, she was in a high state of excitement.

"You stay long in Paris?"

"Three months."

"Le Louvre…hmm. Very *touristique*." It was said almost under his breath.

"Look," she said aggressively, finally turning to look at him. "I'm an artist, or trying to be one. Not that that's any of your business either. Being here is a great opportunity to see the masters. The fact they hang in the Louvre…" She was unreasonably angry. "I want to see everything I can."

"Hey." He said, then whistled softly at her vehemence. They had passed the Rond Point and were headed down the Champs Elysées toward the Place de La Concorde. "What kind of artist?"

"I have a job in a graphic arts business in New York, but that's only the beginning. I do watercolors on my own and am taking a course in oils at night. That's what I really want to do – oils."

"Does your father like you to be a painter?"

"No. He'd love me to be in business – an accountant."

Déols laughed. As they passed the Place de La Concorde, its fountain was spraying water into the street because of a heavy wind.

"*Merde!*" exclaimed Déols as it splashed his car. "Oh, *excusez-moi*. By the way, when does he go again to Moscow?" he said after a pause.

"Why don't you ask the hair bun?"

"Who?"

"His blonde secretary."

He laughed again. "She wouldn't tell me."

"Neither would I."

They had neared the imposing entrance to the ancient royal

residence, containing so many of the world's precious works of art. Déols stopped the car. The motor was running, the car jiggling slightly in disconcerting fashion. Sara uncrossed her legs, surprised by the sudden hiss of silk, and reached for the door handle. Denys Déols leaned forward on the steering wheel, both arms enwrapping it.

"You know, your father is… er… a controversial character. He's mysterious."

"What do you mean?" she said, turning about quickly.

"He doesn't seem to do things through normal channels."

They were nose-to-nose, very close.

"Covert. Unobserved," Déols started, his intensity dissolving as he looked at her. "One has the feeling he's in deep water." His voice faltered.

"What's that supposed to mean?" she said resentfully.

"You've got to admit he's not your average American businessman in Paris," burst from the journalist.

"Of course he's not average. And what do you know American," Sara said angrily, opening the door. "I know you only drove me here to pump me about my father, and I don't appreciate it."

"*Non… non.*" he protested. "That's not true."

"It's true all right." She got out and leaned in the window. "Thanks for the ride. Next time, don't bother."

Denys Déols smiled, then made an illegal U-turn and roared off to the rue de Rivoli, the old car rattling with the increasing speed.

Sara was bristling as she made her way into *La Grande Galerie*. She couldn't seem to concentrate on the display before her. Denys Déols had distracted her. After all, he was obviously only interested in her because she was Saul Mammon's daughter, and she found his innuendoes about her father insulting. Damn Déols, she whispered.

As she walked the length of the enormous hall with its high skylights through which the morning light filtered, the mass of Italian Renaissance art was overwhelming. She sat on a stone bench in the middle of the *Galerie*, trying to absorb her surroundings – to learn from the elegant brush strokes and the rich shadings of color – but the two words, 'Damn Déols' kept surfacing in her mind.

It was after 12:00 o'clock when she finally walked down the massive stairs and out onto the streets of Paris. Along the rue de Rivoli, she idly perused the shop windows of small jewelers and *parfumeurs*. She stopped at *Angélina's* for a hot chocolate, slathered with *crème fraiche*. She even went into the Hotel Meurice just to look at the lobby with its exquisite antiques, trying to refocus. But it didn't work. At least the barrage of French around her made her know conclusively she was nowhere near Manhattan, where she had so longed to be yesterday. And the night before?

She was guilt ridden and angry about Manny. No wonder she been short with Déols in the car. He made her nervous in a new and different way, and his curiosity about her father incensed her. There were other feelings as well that he had set up she could not accept. She didn't want feelings. Damn that man. Damn all of them. DamnDéols. In Sara's vocabulary, it had become one word.

December 19ᵗʰ, 1979

Chapter Nine

Sara came into 17, avenue Foch on this bright winter morning with a spring in her step. She had gone to *Le Drug Store* on the Champs Elysées for American Alka-Seltzer and Ipecac for her father who had returned from Moscow in the middle of the night. He had complained of feeling lousy. What could he expect? He treated Aeroflot like a commuter shuttle.

In spite of his upset stomach, Saul Mammon was enthusiastic about the imminent opening, on Christmas Day, of the new hotel in mid-town Moscow he had been so instrumental in erecting. Built in an unusual crescent shape, The Red Moon's grand opening would kick off a huge, exclusive, public relations campaign by Novikov's people, to be set in motion in the next day or two. The Soviet Union, to capitalize on the event, would invite all-important persons from a number of countries to the luxurious, tourist-oriented new edifice off Red Square. It would be a scoop for <u>Pravda</u> and for the Soviet people. Moscow was to be first with the news, as it stepped forward on the world stage with this magnificent structure.

Would Sara like to accompany her father to this spectacular event, come Christmas Day?

Would she!

She was exhilarated by the walk, eager to get upstairs, back to nursing her father's dyspepsia, and planning the Russian trip. She wore the same dark suit this day with a vivid, Kelly green blouse and matching cap. She carried her drug store purchases in a French string shopping sack and was just finishing off a ham and cheese concoction on a mini-*baguette*, bought at a side booth off the Champs Elysées. It was delectable, the small roll crisp and fresh.

Denys Déols was again on the settee in the entry room. She froze when she saw him, swallowing fast.

He glanced at this watch, folded his newspaper, and stood up. Suddenly he saw her hesitating there. He blocked her way, looking at her from top to toe in that disconcerting manner of his.

"You look *comme une française*" he said admiringly, as she held the last bit of *baguette* at her side.

Sara turned and went into the tiny elevator. Déols followed. She kept her eyes down but could feel him breathing next to her.

"Hungry?" he said with a grin, eyeing the bit of remaining loaf.

She did not reply. "What do you want now?" she said suddenly, looking up at him with a direct gaze.

"I have an appointment with your father."

"Today?" She was astonished.

"He called me this morning."

They did not speak again until they had reached the third floor. She unlocked the apartment door – all the bolts. It took some doing. They seemed more cumbersome that usual. She struggled with them for what seemed too long a time as he leaned against the wall watching.

"Need any help?" he asked, as she stuffed the leftover bread in her bag.

"No thanks."

As the door finally opened, Déols said to her, his voice grave, "I wasn't prepared for you."

"Nor I for you," was her response. She did not dare look at him as she walked quickly down the hall toward her bedroom, anxious to get away from him. She had been so near to him in the elevator, she hadn't been able to breathe right.

Over her shoulder, she saw her father come out of the salon and greet Déols. The two men went into the green and gold room. They left the door ajar. Sara paused halfway down the hall, near a tiger figurine on a pedestal. She was desperately curious. She turned and walked quietly back up the hall. It was so unlike her to eavesdrop, a trait she despised, but she could not resist.

"...raised on the Normandy coast." It was Déols deep voice. "Honfleur." She caught the name of the tiny fishing town as she neared the salon. "I was born in the middle of the worst of World War Two – never knew my father. He was killed at Dunkirk."

It seemed her father was doing the interviewing, not DamnDéols. He was older than he looked, Sara thought as she stood by the partially open door. His words put him in his mid-thirties. And Honfleur. She had been there with her father two years ago after she completed the art school education he would not acknowledge. They had spent a day in Honfleur, before going to the yacht, 'The Ottelia,' in the South.

The voices had ceased in the salon. She could hear the sound of coffee being poured into a cup. Honfleur, she thought, with its minuscule harbor. She remembered the delicate mussels in wine sauce her father and she had shared at a bistro along the quai. Déols had eyes the color of mussel shells, blue-black and shiny.

Now her father's voice was speaking low. She strained to hear. "The hotel in Moscow, sir?" Déols was asking.

"The Red Moon?" her father said. "It was built primarily for the 1980 Olympic games, next summer, a place for the important people to stay." He chuckled. "But soon enough, it will attract general tourism. I put the deal together. I'm very proud of it. It's a multi-national arrangement."

"How so?"

"1700 rooms – outfitted with all French equipment down to the last cognac snifter. On Soviet soil. Western capital. One thousand three hundred Yugoslav and French workmen. What would *you* call it?"

"When does it open?"

"On Christmas Day. A grand opening with dignitaries from all over the world."

"You mean next week?"

"I mean next week. In fact, less than a week from today."

"May I announce that?"

"Be my guest. The scoop's yours."

Sara was stunned. What about the Russsians! Her father had distinctly told her this announcement was supposed to be a Soviet scoop and of their plans to exploit the event with grandeur. He had promised Soviet exclusivity! How could he treat his Russian friends in this manner, to increase his own self-importance?

"They say, sir," Déols continued to her father, "you have close connections with a man named Cutter at the American Embassy."

"True enough. He's an acquaintance, a good connection."

"Is he CIA?"

Her father laughed. "My, oh my. Do you honestly think I'd tell you if I knew?"

"When do you go again to Moscow?"

"In a couple of days. For the opening of The Red Moon."

"You go so frequently to the USSR. May I suggest you're a perfect conduit for the exchange of sensitive information," the reporter said, his words quick, pointed.

"Do you really expect me to respond to that? And who says?" Her father's voice sounded defensive.

Sara turned on her heel and hurried toward her room. She was furious. The revelations about The Red Moon were supposed to be issued in Moscow. How dare her father betray the Russian's trust?

And Déols. The arrogance. What was he hinting at and how stupid of him to ask so boldly. If something secret was going on with Saul Mammon, he would hardly tell a journalist from <u>Le Monde</u>.

Denys Déols had aroused a combination of suspicion, and anger, with her father as the vortex. He had also evoked anticipation. If he was there again tomorrow on that lobby settee...

Coming toward her from her father's bedroom was Renata in a peignoir of mauve silk. It was so sheer, every line of the thin body was revealed, including the two sharp points of her pelvic bones. The two women passed each other preoccupied with their own thoughts.

Sara felt chilled. As she opened the bedroom door, she glanced down the hall as Denys Déols emerged in his raincoat and went toward the foyer. When he reached the entrance, he turned and looked down the length of the corridor as if he were looking for something lost. His eyes found Sara's flushed face. Her gaze held Déols for many seconds. His eyes WERE made of the blue-black mussel shells, she decided as she stood there. Only not hard. She could almost see to the sea through them.

He was not downstairs in the lobby the next morning when she left for La Musée d'Art Moderne in the Pompidou Center to see the Modiglianis. He was not there when she left to go to the Musée Picasso, nor was he sitting rumpled on the settee when she returned after lunch, nor when she went out in the late afternoon to have hot chocolate at *Angélina's*. She wasn't sure she really wanted more decadent cocoa, but she had to see if he was there in the lobby or if his old Citroën was parked on the Avenue Foch. It was not. He was not.

December 20th, 1979

Chapter Ten

On December 20th, the first of Denys Déols articles about Saul Mammon was featured prominently on the first page of <u>Le Monde</u>.

"SAUL MAMMON, THE RED MOON, AND OTHER MYSTERIES" ran the title, in French, of course. Sara found a Larousse dictionary in the bookcase in the salon.

The article started with the blazing announcement of the grand opening of The Red Moon Hotel in Moscow on Christmas Day, with the full details Sara had heard her father give Déols in his interview here in the apartment. There was further discussion of the Olympics to be held in the early summer of 1980 in Moscow, the arenas, the security, but special emphasis was given to the new lush caravansary, The Red Moon, built specifically to impress the Olympic guests next year.

Sara was sprawled on the bed in her bedroom, the newspaper spread before her, dictionary in hand. As she read laboriously, she grew increasingly disturbed. What the Russians must think of the untrustworthiness of her father? Hadn't he promised that they would have the privilege of announcing the opening of the new hotel in their capital to the waiting world? How would Moscow react to his jumping the gun? How could Saul Mammon have leaked this information against the express wishes and rights of his partner?

Sara had trouble translating the piece from the French, but as she managed to get the thrust of the words Denys Déols had written, she began to have trouble seeing the page. Her eyes burned with tears of anger through the contact lenses.

> "Saul Mammon is known for the most imaginative business arrangements. 'If I thought you had an interest in the Taj Mahal,' he told this reporter, 'I'd have no hesitation in going to the Indian Government and saying, Look, I've got this deal.' To Saul Mammon, it's all in a day's work."

Now why did DamnDéols put it that way? What a misleading quote, yet Sara had no doubt her father had said just that in just that way. She read on.

> "'I never quite abandon a connection because eventually it might produce a plum.'"

And another quote:

> "'I had to drag Michelson Frères kicking and screaming to the U.S.S.R.'"

How dare DamnDéols? It was an invasion of privacy, to quote so precisely, Sara thought irrationally. But it was the final paragraph of the article that outraged her.

> "Is the American entrepreneur, Saul Mammon, a shrewd fixer, dependent on cultivating friends in high places?

Or is he a more sinister figure, capable of betraying his colleagues and his country? Or, to be kind, is he simply the ingenious businessman in the rough seas of international finance searching for the perfect deal?"

Sara's mouth fell open. 'A sinister figure.' What kind of scurrilous reporter was this Denys Déols? How did he have the gall? She scrunched the paper into a ball and threw it angrily to the floor. Could she sue? She thought. For what? Innuendo?

Instead, furious, she picked up the telephone.

———

How could she ever have thought him attractive? He was nothing but a snake in the grass. Sara's impatience grew with her anger as she sped across Paris as swiftly as the crazy taxi could take her.

"*Vite, vite*," she urged the ancient driver as she nervously picked at the clasp on her sketchpad. His eyes rolled upward. She saw this reflected in the rear-view mirror, as his tongue barked back at her that he was going as '*vite*' as possible. All Americans always asked the same of him, and they would get there when they got there. It was '*la vie.*'

On the phone earlier this morning, Denys Déols had tersely agreed to meet with her at *L'Aurore*, a bistro adjacent to his office, in the late afternoon. Her fury had only increased with the delay in confronting him. All day she had grown more wild with rage. She could not eat lunch. She could not see pictures. Her eyes were blind with anger. Much less could she sketch.

He was waiting with the ubiquitous newspaper folded on the marble table top, his raincoat slung over the back of the chair, smoking a *Gauloise*. It was a working bistro near the Place de La Bastille, filled, even at this hour, with workmen at the zinc bar having a couple of tots of brandy to ease the end of the workday. They buzzed next to the counter like flies around a honey pot.

Déols' head was down and he was reading. He wore an old sweater with ragged elbows. He did not look at Sara, as she stood there for what felt like at least two minutes. When he did, he stood up with a slow smile growing on his lips, his eyes genuine in their welcome. It only infuriated her further that the warmth of his lips matched that in his eyes, when many peoples' don't.

She sat down abruptly. In a charcoal gray coat, with a pale blue turtleneck jersey rising in a cowl at her throat, Sara had the full attention of the man before her.

His attention. At first, that had been all she wanted, not this admiration. The shine in his eyes put her on edge.

He ordered her a *café* and another for himself.

"Why do you hate my father?" Sara blurted out, after a tense moment of sipping coffee that was much too hot.

"I don't hate him."

"That article - your implications that he might sell out his country. You don't call that hate?"

"I'm only a reporter. I tell the things I see. Your father is *un mystère*. They were only questions, you know. I had to raise them."

"It's libel. You have no proof."

"There's a famous American attorney living here in Paris. He's an authority on East-West trade. I have his quote somewhere." He was flipping through a small notebook. "Ah." he said, squinting to read his own writing. "'Saul Mammon has a tendency to be involved with two sides of every equation, yet he's always able to supply the missing ingredient to make the deal.'" Déols glanced up with a canny look. Sara resented it.

"What does that prove? He keeps on both sides of an issue – aware of what's going on. What's so bad about that?" Yet, all she could think of was MGM and the man from Quebec, the enemy in her father's living room, giving information, as Saul had told her about on the plane.

"Whispers of a KGB connection follow him everywhere, since he started going back and forth to Moscow so often."

"Whispers," she said, furious. "Nothing more."

"*Mon Dieu.* It's been since 1972," said Déols, his animation rising. "Every other week or so, with the blue jeans and the soybeans and who knows what all. He bargains with the Russians," he went on relentlessly.

"So what?"

"Everyone knows the Russians shade the truth. Does he shade it, too?"

"He's smarter. He says they like a 'leader,'" she said proudly.

"The Russians lie to everyone. How come they trust him?"

"Because..."

He pointed a finger at her. "You try to defend your father with no defenses at all. Let me ask you, what hold does he have over them that other world-class businessmen haven't?"

"I don't know."

Denys Déols was stopped by her expression. Her face had suddenly crumpled like paper.

"I love my father." It was a whisper.

"That's obvious," he said slowly.

"I need my father." Sara lowered her eyes. The corners of her mouth were drawn down in a kind of anguish. "I need to...know him..."

"But that's no reason to love everything about him, and everything he does," the newspaperman said gently.

"Of course it is. Love...loving should mean accepting that person with all his faults."

"But not necessarily approving all his actions, particularly if they are dangerous."

"You don't understand. My father and I. It's special. It's different."

"Not that different," he interrupted. "Only perhaps, for a daughter, you're just a little bit more than most like a poodle on a leash."

"A poodle." Sara bridled. "A poodle. Then you're the bulldog. He's the bone you gnaw on, my poor father."

"Poor he's not."

A crashing, nervous silence descended upon both of them. Sara poured more coffee from the little *filtre* in front of her. Her hands shook as she diddled with her coffee cup. Why didn't she just get up and leave? Instead, she seemed to be part of the bentwood chair.

"You keep looking at me," she said finally.

"Can't help it."

There was a palpable silence between them. They were oblivious to the zinc bar, which still hummed with activity.

"I'm scared for him," she said suddenly, tears pricking her eyes.

"Better be scared OF him," Déols said not unkindly. "You must admit... *il manque de* ... he's maybe...er... unethical."

Sara turned white, as a tear slowly dropped into her coffee cup. She hastily brushed at her eyes with the back of her hand.

"I'm sorry," he said. "I just don't want you to get hurt."

"I'll look out for myself."

"You can't be objective."

"And you can, I suppose."

"No," he said slowly. "I guess maybe not, not where you're concerned."

They came out of the bistro into the late afternoon light and stood on the cobblestone pavement. The traffic hurtled from the conjoining streets into the semi-square on which La Bastille had stood, but their eyes were not on the bustle of cars, nor on the monument in the center of La Place de La Bastille across the way. They were fixed on each other.

On Déols face was an expression of sudden discovery. Unconsciously, she seemed to invite him to a romantic communion. She was acutely aware of it, this sensuality that streamed from her. It was there, as was the anguish about her father that pulled at the corners of her mouth.

"That was the Bastille, over there," he said, tilting his head across the street, their eyes locked.

She nodded limply under his gaze.

"The people of Paris stormed it in 1789." He sounded like the cab driver, rattling at her.

"July 14th," she said tonelessly.

"You know our history." He seemed surprised.

"DamnDéols. Everybody knows that." He had to bend to hear her response.

They stood there, stuck on the cobblestones. Then, he brusquely grabbed her hand and pulled her down the street after him.

In silence they arrived at the door of his studio-like apartment on rue de La Chapelle, not far from La Place de La Bastille. The room they entered was dark, although daylight still beamed outside.

Through the dimness, she could see they were at the entrance of his sitting room. He turned on a lamp. "Here. You need a drink," he said, making for a bottle of brandy on a small bureau against one wall that served as a bar.

Sara looked around her at the unkempt room full of books and bachelor belongings.

"Sit down," he said, nodding his head in the direction of a lumpy couch covered in paisley. She wriggled out of her coast, suddenly awkward. What am I doing here? she thought, but quite mute, she sat awkwardly on the couch, still clutching the sketch pad. He came to sit beside her, handing her a wine glass of brandy.

"You mustn't get so upset," he said sipping from his own.

"God, how can I not be upset," she said suddenly vehement, glaring at him.

"Truth is hard."

"Truth indeed," she said.

"That's what I try for," he said calmly.

The sat side by side on the uncomfortable couch, Sara's leather pumps neatly pointed straight forward.

Denys Déols touched the sketchbook on her lap. "May I look?"

"Be my guest," she said primly.

"*Eh?*"

"Sure. Go ahead."

He took the sketchpad and undid the clasp, opening the pages, leafing through.

"Ah – Les Jardins des Tuileries," he said. "These are really quite good," he said thoughtfully.

"Glad you approve," she said, but she was secretly pleased he at least recognized the venue.

"You did all these?"

"Oh, there're lots more"

"They have a quality. Very modern." Then turning to her, he said, "You have a quality too." His face was close. She could smell his breath, smoky and sweet.

She moved from him a little. "Oh, I'd like so much to be good," she said wistfully.

"Oh, you're good all right." He looked again at the sketches. "Art's interesting. I don't... I don't have much education in it. I just know what I like." He looked at her again.

Sara, looked at him, speaking quickly, totally unnerved by this conversation. "Well... I... to me...I mean art's instinctive, don't you think? I try not to think too much. I try to feel."

Déols nodded his head and reached for her lips with his own, smiling a little, placing one hand on the side of her cheek. It felt soft against her skin, then a simple kiss, but with such promise. She pulled away. "*Hst*," he said, again reaching for her mouth, his own lips shiny and curved with desire. Sara lay in his arms as he kissed and stroked her, but it went no further.

He stood up beside the couch. "Are you hungry?"

She looked up shocked. Food was hardly on her mind. Shame swept over her. She did not even know this man, and here she was, eager for him, this betrayer of her father, but his lips, the smell of his hair, the force of his tongue. She stumbled into her coat, unable to speak. After turning out the lamp, Déols went to the door. She stood in the dark. She could hear him breathing.

"Coming?" he asked, as the hall light slanted abruptly across the room. She followed him down the stairs and out onto rue de la Chapelle.

Chapter Eleven

He took her around the corner into a local Brasserie called *La Muniche*. In front of the place, a pair of oyster shuckers plied their trade right there in the street.

Denys Déols said a cheery "*bon soir*" to the two men who grinned and said the equivalent of "*ooh la la*" as Sara swept past. The restaurant was noisy and crowded, but they found a small table at the back. "You must have the oysters. They're as fresh as any in Paris," he said, ordering a large carafe of white wine. "And *La Muniche* is famous for its *choucroute*. It's spectacular. Would you like that?"

She nodded. What the hell was she doing here with this arrogant man who had started something so physical, then taken her to this unromantic place that smelled of sauerkraut?

"What does your father think of your art? Does he look at your pictures?" he said, digging into the massive *huitres*, dripping with briny juice.

"I don't think he cares much one way or the other," she said defensively. "He prefers other forms of pleasure." She blushed. Déols grinned at her.

"Yes," he said, attacking another oyster. "Your father certainly doesn't like to…how do you Americans put it…'rough it.'"

"I guess I am one who did <u>not</u> come up the hard way."

"Perhaps it was harder than you're willing to admit." He looked at her directly.

"I sometimes think, there Saul Mammon goes, figuring out his next move," she said. "And somehow I'm in it. Even at a distance, it's always my turn. I've got to perform. I feel like some sort of lightening rod for his expectations."

"I've got expectations too," Déols said suggestively, and Sara blushed again.

The *choucroute* arrived, mounds of sauerkraut and sausage and pig's feet and braised pork. It smelled of beer and caraway. Déols ate with gusto, but through the noisy dinner, Sara was hot, restless. She picked at the food.

"What's the matter with you?" Déols said, genuinely concerned at her silence as he finished his meal, wiped his lips and laid down his fork.

"Nothing."

"Oh yes, Sara. There's something." He tilted his head to one side. "Is it because I kissed you?"

She turned purple. "How dare you."

"You didn't seem to mind."

"After all you've written."

"Look, Sara, my *métier* is my passion. My job comes before anything else. I'm sorry but it's the way I am."

"Then why did you kiss me?"

"What do you mean, why?" He shook his head. "You Americans!"

"Why?"

"Well…you…you're a …well, you're beautiful and interesting."

"No. I mean why did you stop?" she whispered.

Déols' jaw dropped. He threw his head back and laughed.

"I want to go back to your apartment." She could not believe she was saying this. It was as if another voice spoke.

"Why?" he said with a twinkle.

"I want you to touch me again," she said angrily.

"Where? he said.

"All over"

"Ah," he said, summoning the *garçon*. *"L'addition, s'il vous plaît."*

They arrived back at his apartment, rushing, although Sara's limbs were so heavy with longing, she could hardly walk. As Déols shut the door behind them, he pulled her to him, leaning against the door jamb in the darkened sitting room. Any silhouette they presented was one of a single being, his head bent down to her lips, his arms around her, bearing down, a weight that buckled her knees. He undid every button on the gray coat, one by one. She could barely see his fingers in the dimness as they struggled with each, and she wondered what the buttons were made of. The coat fell to the floor.

He took her to his bed, leading her by the hand. She was not sure how she got there. She only knew she felt airborne. From the beginning, it was a battle between them, a battle he won. His control infuriated her, as she repeatedly lost her own to the heat generated by his lack of inhibition and his confidence.

At first, Saul Mammon seemed to be in bed with them. Denys was pitiless with Sara. It seemed to her he felt he could subdue Saul Mammon through his daughter. She discovered Denys Déols was almost as obsessed with her father as was she. She sought to diminish her lover's aggressiveness by reaching for him repeatedly with mouth and hand. As the battle progressed and they became more languorous, Denys was able to take the time to explore her body in the light of the bedside lamp "You're beautiful," he breathed

"Ah no," she said. "My looks…are so dark…"

"Dark and lush," he whispered. "I don't know if Eve were light or dark, but if such a woman as you had stood in the garden, the apple would surely have been eaten."

With this, tears stung her eyes. She pulled him to her and clung to the length of his body desperately. He could feel her tears on his own cheeks. Her vulnerability was like an open wound, and it touched the heart of the rather callous, experienced Frenchman.

Up to these moments, Sara had been caught in a webbed trap. With each caress, each kiss on her lips, Denys seemed to wipe away the strings that ensnared her. He was beginning to unravel the lattice. It like unwrapping a mummy, freeing her spirit from the confusion of feelings of the last days, of the suspicions and fears, of the Mannys and of the gold, of the Renatas and Novikovs, and most of all of Saul Mammon.

His black eyes held her transfixed. "DamnDéols…DamnDéols," she murmered. He kissed her mouth. She smelled of herself and of him, and it tasted of something primal from the sea, saline and delicious, the taste of caviar. He fell asleep beside her. She remained still, letting her heart subside.

Lying there, she visualized Denys Déols, the man beside her. His eyes were indeed the color of those blue black shells. Reflected in them was the windy coast near Honfleur, the old port where the Seine meets the sea. He was the boy who had lost his father at Dunkirk, and not just a hard-nosed Paris newspaperman after all. At this moment, she naively believed that after this night she would now have some control over his crusade against Saul Mammon, and that she had won something far beyond this particular engagement.

She managed to extricate herself from his arms, rolling him off to his side, without awakening him. She got up from the bed, found her clothes scattered from one end of the place to the other. Her hands shook as she dressed, stumbling about the apartment as noiselessly as possible. He did not make a sound. In the light of the one lamp in the bedroom, she began to see his live-a-day world; the large bed in disarray with a dozen pillows, a half-full cup of coffee on the radiator, the typewriter on the desk in the dimness of the small sitting room, the bar-bureau with its bottles of brandy and red wine, the lumpy couch in the center, books askew on their shelves, a pile of magazines and newspapers folded on the floor next to the desk.

Sara slipped down the stairs and found a taxi over by *La Muniche*. The oyster shuckers were gone, but the odor of the brine remained in the cool night air. DamnDéols. She was still furious with his pursuit of the truth about Saul Mammon, but what a loving man was he!

After this night, she had blunted the attack, she was sure. She smiled. 'My *métier* is my passion,' he had said. "We'll see about that," she whispered to herself. Perhaps she had diverted some of that passion to herself.

She stepped from the car at number 17, avenue Foch and stood for a moment under the streetlight. The taxi driver was looking at her with admiration. She smiled at him as he drove off toward the glowing Champs Elysées.

"DamnDéols," she said softly, shaking her head, squaring her shoulders as she entered the building. Denys had found her beautiful.

Chapter Twelve

"Christ, Saul. Why doesn't it bother you? That bastard, Déols, practically accuses you of being a traitor!" Sara heard Manny's voice at a high pitch in the green and gold salon as she entered the floral foyer. Her body felt lean and loose, but hearing the strident voice, the heaviness of spirit she had briefly lost seemed to descend upon her once more. She stood for a moment in the foyer, smoothing out the wrinkles in the skirt of her gray coat, which had fallen to the floor at Denys' apartment.

"You're being awfully cavalier, Saul," Ephraim was saying.

"I've been called worse things by better men than Déols," came her father's calm voice. "So have you."

"Not me, Saul. You."

"This article in a daily paper, yet, it's peanuts." She could hear the slam of the newspaper as her father whacked the desk with it. "It's only publicity, a minor publicity, and any publicity is GOOD publicity. Only adds to the mystique."

"Mystique," Manny roared. "The Russians love your new mystique so much, they cancelled the opening of The Red Moon on Christmas Day."

Oh no! Sara thought, shocked, and yes, disappointed.

Manny was still shouting. "Déols' article and the news of the hotel has spawned telecasts…radio broadcasts. Its been picked up by other papers. Mystique, indeed." She could hear Manny's short footsteps pacing. "You pulled the rug from under them on The Red Moon, Saul. That's why they're sending so many 'flattering' telexes. Christ, the telex machine is having a nervous breakdown."

Her father laughed.

"Why'd you do it Saul?" Manny went on.

"Whose hotel is it anyway?" her father said angrily. "The Russians would never have gotten around to it without me."

"Well, now they're after your head."

"You're scaring me to death," her father said this with another laugh.

"You're going to queer all those lucrative Olympic franchise deals if you're not careful. I guarantee it. We'll all be out." There was silence. Then Manny continued firmly, "Well, you'll just have to go to Moscow and make it up to them."

"Be called on the carpet? Not on your life."

"You can talk your way out of anything, Saul," Ephraim interjected.

"You're asking me to kiss ass?"

Sara had reached the entrance and stood just inside the green and gold salon. The three men were spread around the room in varying degrees of tension. They each had a brandy snifter half-filled with the dark liqueur. They all looked at her.

Renata took up the entire loveseat, her feet elevated on the arm, shoes off, magenta toenails twitching, a liqueur glass balanced on her stomach. In her white costume, stirrup pants and body stocking in cream wool, she looked like a pale plank. Sara had a flash vision of red pubic hair beneath the clothing, like a lurid knot in the wood of the board, drawing the eye, her father's eye.

"Look who finally decided to come home," Renata said lazily, puffing on her cigarette. "Well." She sat up, studying Sara. "You look like you just got laid."

Sara flushed. She knew her hair looked extra full. The curls had gotten so tangled, it had been difficult to get a brush through them. Her skin felt tautly drawn, her face cool.

"It would occur to you," she mumbled in response.

"Where've you been?" Manny asked possessively.

She ignored him.

"Did you eat kid?" Her father leaned back in his chair, at the small, leather-tooled desk.

She nodded as she walked across the room to him under Renata's sharp gaze. She kissed him on the forehead. His skin was like ice. In spite of his bold words, this was a reaction of fear. She studied his face. His cheeks beneath the lenses of his glasses were ashen. The mouth, usually turned up with a cherubic turn to the lips or spread in a wide, rakish grin, looked drawn. His jaw had a slight tic as if he clenched his teeth.

What she had just heard him say was simply bravura. As Sara stood there looking down at him, she asked herself, 'Am I the traitor? Is the man with whom I've just made love the enemy, the one for my father to confound?' She wanted to escape to her room. "My feet hurt, I think I'll hit the sack."

"Sleep, kid," her father said affectionately.

"Oh, she will," said Renata, flopping back on the loveseat. "She will." She gave her raucous little laugh.

Sara hurried down the hall. She locked the bedroom door behind her, undressed quickly and lay deep in the bed, her faced rolled into the pillow. Muscles she had never known she owned had been stretched out deliciously. Now she was reminded of what Denys had done to her and she to him. She had cupped his body with her two hands. Her legs had wound around him with a new and tender joy. She fell asleep with the memory of holding him, unable to face the untenable place where she found herself between two such polarized men: Saul Mammon and Denys Déols.

She awoke in a cold sweat. It was near dawn and Saul Mammon had taken over. She had been dreaming under the linen sheets, but not of love. The dream was a triptych, in three sections, her father in all three, his presence so dominant, it completely blocked out the sensual memories of Denys.

In the first part, Saul Mammon's adult face was there with permanent calipers attached like antlers. He was surrounded, an animal in an evil thicket, the bushes of which were made of Renata's hair; in the second part, her father, still with the antlers, was spraying GOLD SHAMPOO in arcs and circles, sitting in a Jacuzzi bathtub in a business suit; the third had his high-speed sports car going over a cliff, all it's tires flying in every direction. Her father was in the front seat screaming.

She had been soundlessly screaming too. Saul Mammon was in danger. She knew it. She was afraid for him because he had cheated. That was the word Manny had used. "It's unwise to cheat the Russians," he had told her father in his office.

Saul Mammon's ego, his need to excite people with new information ahead of the pack was perhaps only the first glint of a Russian iceberg. Denys Déols had hinted at KGB connections and the CIA. Certainly when her father last went to Russia he had come back feeling ill. Did they put something in his food?

Sara's fears for her father escalated. Even softhearted Ephraim had announced Saul Mammon had "wiggled Israel" at the dinner table, the night of her father's emotional striptease. Manny claimed he was doing the same with the Russians.

With each thought Sara ticked off, her body grew colder. She rose and put on the white robe. She walked down the shadowy hall, knees shaking, toward her father's room. The corridor seemed endless. At his door, she paused, holding her breath.

Renata might be in there, in his bed with her red pubic tuft. She pressed her ear to the crack of the door. No sound came from within. As she slowly opened the door, the dim night light from the hall cast a wedge-shaped triangle across the brown rug. She looked toward the bed. It was empty and smooth. With a bold but trembling hand, she threw open the door farther, then quickly turned on the indirect headboard lights which shone down on the brown velvet coverlet. The room was deathly silent, the French doors closed. Where was he? Had he returned to Moscow in the middle of the night to appease his partners? Would they accept his blandishments or would they demand retribution, hurt him, or worse?

She stood frozen in the center of her father's bedroom in a panic, her mind and heart racing. Was there some dreadful omen in the dreams? She could feel her fear. She could smell it emitting from the bushy thicket of her nightmare.

Or was the odor that filled her nostrils the scent of evil, not just fear? Why did her father seem so surrounded by swirling vaporous evil? Did the odor of evil exude from him? Then how was he so successful with people, at least for a time, until the evil mists overcame them? Could other people, besides herself smell it too?

Sara stood there in the forbidding room, desperate to the save the father whose danger had roused her from sleep. If he was in danger, then so was she, for if anything happened to him, he would no longer exist, and she would never know herself.

She tried to focus on his endearing smile, the quickness of tongue that could turn a simple event into a moment of mirth and delight. But she knew it was the other side of him that had put him in danger; his lips set grimly, eyes hard, and the tongue suddenly a sword with a cutting edge. One never knew which Saul Mammon was at home on a given day.

With a cry of anguish, Sara fled the room, running headlong down the hall in the clutch of unreasoning foreboding.

December 21, 1979

Chapter Thirteen

The next afternoon, Sara sat in the salon sketching. She was groggy, troubled by her portentous night.

"Who did you sleep with?" Manny had come into the room silently. His remark startled her. She had not seen him enter. Her head was bent over a charcoal sketch she was drawing, a new picture of her father's face. She turned in her seat on the sofa, grateful that the coffee table was between Manny and herself. "What?"

"You heard me. Who did you sleep with?"

"What a question"

"As Renata noticed last night, you looked like you just, 'had been.'"

"Had been what?"

"Laid."

Sara managed to laugh. "Oh Manny. Consider the source."

"I am. If anyone would know, it's Renata."

"What would you do if I told you? Tell Daddy?"

"Depends."

"He'd never believe you," she said, closing her sketchpad. She did not want Manny to see her father's portrait. She put it carefully on the couch. "Daddy would laugh," she said, consciously echoing Manny's earlier words to her. "He'd think you were crazy." She stood up. "Aren't I attractive enough for it?"

Manny looked flustered. "Who?" he demanded.

"Who what?" She was enjoying the tease. Then she said, slowly. "Manny, some people make love. Others, like you, do sex. You have to be top dog for a couple of seconds."

She walked around him and went down the hall toward the bedroom with unhurried steps, carrying her sketchpad loosely under her arm. The moment she entered, she locked the door behind her.

The thought of two such disparate sexual encounters, one with the loathsome little lawyer, the other with the French journalist haunted her. But the idea of Déols, that she needed him to wipe away the tentacles and dreams that waved across her consciousness, she resented.

Sara had to escape the scene at avenue Foch, at least for a little while. It was late afternoon, but the shops were open because of the coming Christmas holiday. Christmas! She decided to shop for a few presents. As her father evidently had gone on some Persian carpet to the Kremlin, she had an open evening. She would treat herself to dinner in Paris.

She threw on her gray coat and rushed out of the apartment, through the lobby downstairs and found a taxi in the soft dusk at the corner of avenue Kléber, which took her directly to Sulka's. There she bought the first of her Christmas presents. It was for Denys Déols, a handsome sweater to replace the one where the elbows had broken through. Now, why did I do that! she thought.

For her father, she purchased a digital clock that showed the time all over the world. He probably owned one already. Saul Mammon was always way ahead of the game as far as adult toys were concerned. Then there was Renata. After all, she was living with him. Sara found a little fake-jewelry store on the Champs Elysées, next to *Fouquet's*, where she planned to dine. After searching through piles of glitter, she selected a set of psychedelic purple beads, ropes of them, the better to conceal what there was of Renata's bosom and to encircle the skinny neck. The beads were appropriate, they were so vulgar.

With her three packages on the floor at her feet, she sat near the entrance to *Fouquet's* over a Campari and soda, awaiting the veal chop *Normande* she had ordered, watching the glow and bustle along the broad avenue before her. Church bells caroled out in soft dissonance and a bit of extra shine twinkled in the shop windows. Christmas in Paris seemed more serious than in the United States.

The holiday had always been problematic for Daddy. She had always known the Christmas celebration was only for her mother and herself. Her Jewish grandmother disapproved, despite her father's efforts. Sara remembered vividly when Saul gave his mother as a Christmas present, an antique music box. She returned it to him accusing him of jumping to the 'winning side.' When Sara thought of it now, this was precisely what defined Saul Mammon's character.

Suddenly, her thoughts turned bitter as the beautiful dinner arrived. Her father was in Moscow – again! – singing the Russians some erroneous song. How he loved the game of making people believe he could get them whatever they wanted. But this time, it was he on the carpet over The Red Moon fiasco. God help him.

Stop it, Sara, she said to herself. I don't want to sink into the Mammon-trap over my veal in brandied cream. But there seemed to be no help for it. She pushed the dish away, paid the check, and walked slowly back to 17, avenue Foch.

December 22, 1979

Chapter Fourteen

The headline ran: "THE SOVIET UNION, SAUL MAMMON, AND OTHER MYSTERIES," byline Denys Déols. Paris, December 22, 1979, all in French.

> "'Like you eat an elephant. Bite by bite,'" Saul Mammon replied, when asked how he dealt with the Russians."

What in blazes does that mean, 'bite by bite,' Sara thought. Here she was again in her bedroom, trying to decipher Denys Déols' French interpretation of her father's words and it annoyed her. The first paragraph continued:

> "This brilliant American entrepreneur, known in some circles for his deviousness, has been nibbling away at Russia for the past seven years."

Ha! Daddy's not so dumb. You have to nibble away, no matter how large the monster.

"The latest and most spectacular bites are, first, the franchise arrangements with American companies – printers, flag manufacturers, food and liquor concessionaires—for the 1980 Olympic Games to be held in Moscow next August. Second, with Chapin Euro-Tel, Ltd., the erection of a new, grand hotel, The Red Moon, off Red Square, to house the Olympic guests." (See Le Monde, December 20, 1979).

How Sara's heart would have burst with pride, if she could have been there for the grand opening. Sara, not Renata, was to have been Saul Mammon's companion at the glittering ceremony on Christmas day that her father had sabotaged.

"James Chapin, founder of Chapin Euro-Tel, Ltd., one of the world's largest hotel chains, is no longer available to Saul Mammon. The two men had a falling out over finances during the construction of The Red Moon."

Now why does Déols have to bring that up? Sara pounded the bed pillow with her fist in anger.

"Saul Mammon has bragged that he has helped three hundred Soviet Jews emigrate to Israel. 'When I hear that Saul Mammon is concerned about Russia's Jews, I smile. He is interested in only one thing. Money,' James Chapin remarked with bitterness."

Damn Chapin. What a crass thing to say. Her father wanted to promote peace – "to do his bit for it" - through business. He had said so often enough.

But Déols wasn't through with his diatribe.

"A top-notch Israeli member of the Knesset who prefers to remain anonymous, says, 'Saul Mammon is no friend to Israel.' He would comment no further, but did proclaim that the Israelis are in possession of a letter found in the captured files of Idi Amin, thanking Mammon for arranging a ten million dollar Soviet arms shipment to Uganda. In the same cache, there is evidence of Soviet arms sales to Libya and the PLO, through Mammon, that indicates he may be charging Russia and its customers double commissions."

Sara found Déols' insinuations outrageous, but she was compelled to finish reading.

"Saul Mammon professes that 'No one listens to a poor man,' and his life style indicates he believes this firmly. 'It's as easy to play at the top as it is at the bottom,' he claims. His daughter and only child is beneficiary of this largesse, but somehow, she is his touch with humanity. Saul Mammon claims his daughter as his 'eternity.'"

She was stunned. It was beyond belief, that Denys Déols would bring her into his vendetta against Saul Mammon, use her own father's words – his personal words to HER. Déols was an arrogant, self-serving, two bit journalist.

"'When you get a deal that's so complex it turns everybody else off, try me,' is just another premise of Saul Mammon's. Anyone who accepts that challenge had better have courage and a strong stomach."

———

It was dusk. Sara had been sitting on the stoop in front of Denys Déols' apartment building for what seemed like hours. She had buzzed and buzzed at the massive black door with no success. Now she sat huddled on the rim of the doorstep. The edge of stone beneath her buttocks was pointed, but not nearly so sharp as her thoughts of the journalist. His second article on Saul Mammon had outraged her more than the first. His quotes of her father's intimate words to her on board the Concorde seemed a gross violation of confidence. She had told Déols of this – the word 'eternity' – in a private sentimental moment – in bed, in fact. He had used it in his newspaper. She felt diminished. His passion had not been diverted from his *métier* to her, as she had wished. She had absolutely no control over this man.

She stood up and peered through the twilight in both directions, trying to spot the tall, slopping figure of DamnDéols. What if he was with another girl, some other patsy as grist for his mill of innuendo and accusation?

And there he was, ambling up the street in his old raincoat, head down, reading as he walked, his dark hair untidy as always.

She flew at him, almost knocking him over. He didn't see her coming and he reeled back, raising his arms before his face as she pummeled his chest. They struggled there in the street, he clutching at the flailing arms and small figure that was upon him.

"You know, you're strong. *Dieu*… Eh..quiet now," he said, gentling her as he would a nervous horse.

"How could you," she said to him brokenly, moving back, fists still clenched. "How could you?"

"What?" he said solemnly.

"You used what I told you. You've been using me all the time."

"How using you?"

"To get at my father. What I told you was in good faith."

"And I repeated it in good faith. After all, you are the best thing about Saul Mammon. You make him human."

"You used me, Déols."

"I feel used too," he said abruptly

"You?"

"Why did you just creep out on me two nights ago like some little thief in the night, *hein* ?"

"I was ashamed."

"Ah, you Americans. So ashamed of sex."

"Not sex. Ashamed because you have a vendetta against Saul Mammon and I had…we had…"

"Made love?" he said, finishing her sentence.

Tears of rage streamed down her face. She could not speak.

"Oh…oh, Sara," he said, genuinely concerned. "Please don't."

He tried to touch her, but she kept backing away until she was pressed against the black door of his building. He unlatched it as she tried to control herself. He put a hand beneath her elbow and guided her, stumbling, to the stairs. They walked up the two flights slowly, Sara as if she were an old lady. She could hardly see the steps.

In his sitting room, he sat her on the lumpy couch, went to the bar-bureau and picked up a bottle of red wine and a couple of glasses. This gave her a moment to become enraged anew. By the time he turned and faced her, she was on her feet, quivering with an anger she didn't know she possessed.

"No wine. No nothing from you. Don't try to placate me."

"Ah, Sara," he said, standing there, hands filled with the bottle and glasses. "Just because we have a sexual affair, it doesn't mean I stop being a journalist. It's my calling – to try to write the truth."

"You won't even admit you wrote lies about my father, making him look like some venal, money-hungry, subversive traitor! Well, I know who the real Benedict Arnold is. It's you. Déols, it's you." And she was at him again, beating his chest, head down, pounding the rain-coated shoulders, scratching at his face. Denys dropped the glasses and the bottle of wine. They broke on the floor in a spray of shards and voluptuous red liquor. In desperation, he lifted her up in the air as she wriggled against him, and threw her on the lumpy couch, he on top of her, pinning her hands and finally her mouth with his own. She continued to wriggle.

Still in his raincoat, he began to move against her through the layers of clothing. He held her wrists tight. In spite of her anger, she willed him to not let go. And then they were kissing deeply, both lost. There was nothing gentle in the way he took her, nor in her own responses. He tore at her underclothes, as she cried out and then, it was just Denys and Sara.

December 23, 1979

Chapter Fifteen

Sara awoke near dawn in Denys' arms and bed. She shut her eyes as he stirred against her and touched her hair in his sleep. It was the gentlest gesture he had yet made toward her, but even as this moment passed, she could feel the nagging, ungracious thoughts. She disentangled herself, put on his sweater with no elbows. The sweater was long. It held the smell of him like an embrace. She pushed the arms of the sweater way up because the sleeves hung below her hands, and went into the tiny kitchen to make a *filtre*.

As she waited for the coffee to drip through, what had been a kind of acceptance was now giving way to a taste more like defeat. She had capitulated. Again, DamnDéols had won, in spite of her rage at his personal attacks on her father. These last hours, there had been no further words about Saul Mammon, but through the shared intimacy and passion, Sara's conviction about her father's innocence began to crumble. Whether she liked it or not, Déols and she were now allied in a common pursuit of the truth about her father. Through the physical coupling, an unspoken commitment had been made, a cathartic for her, perhaps a crusade for him.

She had to admit that some of her own instincts about Saul

Mammon matched Denys Déols' facts. She was beginning to see her father through his eyes.

The coffee tasted bitter. She added a little of the bluish French milk to make it more palatable. If only she could dilute her feelings for Denys. Her loyalties to Saul Mammon were compromised, and this engendered a rage toward the journalist.

Her thoughts would not be kept submerged, as she sat in the little kitchen. Manny with his voracious ways insinuated himself into her consciousness. She had enticed him. She had brought the whole Manny problem upon herself by trying to provoke her father to take notice of her. She had blatantly tried to compete sexually, to pull his attention away from Renata, as that woman fed Saul Mammon with whipped cream and chocolate on the evening of that awful dinner. Shame made Sara's cheeks flush.

A vindictive venom toward Manny spread through her. He was to blame, not she. He hovered over her waiting to drop upon her without warning.

Suddenly with a cry, Sara jumped up from the wire-back chair on which she had been sitting. "I've got it," she said in a loud whisper.

"You've got what?" Denys was leaning against the doorjamb, face sleepy, hair rumpled and so sensuous looking, her knees grew weak. She went over to him and they embraced, leaning against the wall.

"What have you got?"

She looked up at him. "An idea."

"Have you got coffee, too?"

She nodded, extricated herself from his arms and brought him a cup, half coffee, half milk.

He sat in one of the two wire-backed chairs that seemed to fill the tiny room. "An idea?" he said lazily.

"I want you to do a favor for me."

He looked wary. "A favor for you or for your father?"

"It's for me."

He smiled and yawned. *"Eh bien ..."*

"Have you met Manny Kiser?"

Denys thought a moment. "I've seen him, just once, at your father's office. I was waiting outside, as usual." He made a little grimace. "Why?"

"I want you to write about him in <u>Le Monde.</u>"

"Manny Kiser? But why?"

"He's, well, he's done something…to me…and…." Sara's voice trailed off.

"You want to get even, eh?"

"Well, he deserves it."

"Now who is using who?"

"You owe me," she said after a pause.

"I do not owe you. I wrote what I believe to be the truth. You have nothing to do with it."

"Manny and Daddy have been linked together for years," she said, trying to pique his curiosity. "He's been my father's confidante, knows where the bones are buried."

"Why?"

"Why what?"

"Why do you so earnestly wish me to write about him, bring him into this, not that it might not make an interesting sidebar. He's a smart fellow, expedient. Why do you wish to publicly lay him open?"

"I told you. He did something." Sara stopped speaking. She paced the little space, in and out between the chairs. She had to step over Denys' feet. Then, she went on, "you don't understand. Manny thinks what he knows about my father could put Daddy in the Federal Penitentiary for a hundred years. Something about taxes." She was growing enthusiastic. "But in an American Court of Law, you know Saul Mammon would get off with a hand slap."

"I doubt that," Denys interrupted dryly.

"My father's connections reach all the way to the White House," she said defiantly. "Manny's the one who would get life in prison."

Denys laughed. "Ah, Sara, Manny Kiser may be a compulsive, driven, little man, perhaps, but he is – how do you say –a small fish."

"No. Really," she said, facing him, hands on hips. "Manny does the dirty work."

"Saul Mammon's hatchet man?"

"I've heard…I've heard Manny's capable of terrible things." Sara's voice trembled.

"On whose orders? Your father's?"

"Well, my father never took an oath before the Bar Association!" Even in her own mind, this sounded ridiculous.

Denys was watching her closely. "You want to expose Manny Kiser – for some mysterious reason, eh?" There was a long pause. "Then why not the man who pulls the strings? Why the small fish and not the shark?"

"DamnDéols," she burst out. "Manny has a lot to lose," she said vehemently, getting a second wind. "He has a fancy New York law practice and through my father, lots of international clients, too – Herman Tyson, the Texas oilman – James Chapin from London. Why, Manny's just written a high-toned book on jurisprudence in America."

Denys stood up. He moved to her and put his hands on her shoulders. Looking down at her seriously, he said, *"Ma belle* Sara. Don't do this. Do you know, all at once, you begin to look a lot like Saul Mammon?" He turned quickly and left her standing there in the middle of the room.

She felt all the blood leave her face. Denys' words seemed to echo in the small space. She hugged herself, arms crossed over her breasts in his homely sweater.

"I don't want to look like Saul Mammon or act like Saul Mammon or think like Saul Mammon," she repeated to herself in a whisper as she slowly sank to the floor between the two wire-backed chairs.

Getting back at Manny suddenly didn't seem such a fine idea after all. Worse, she could not bear to think that even unconsciously she had tried to use a man like Denys Déols in this fashion, as her father surely would. "Hold them close. Grapple them to you with hoops of steel. But love them up," he had once told her. "They should never feel the shiv."

Sara sat on the floor, mute. Denys returned. He was dressed in another sweater and slacks.

He saw her despair. He came to her without a word, crouched beside her and gently helped her to her feet.

"*Allons-y,*" he said firmly. "Let's get out of here."

Chapter Sixteen

I t was a morning with puffy clouds, a streaming sun and the flat green land of the Île de France. Denys Déols drove Sara in the Citroën past the cranes dredging the river Seine, past the Ponts, with Nôtre Dame in the distance and St. Chapelle, their gargoyles and spires rising.. There was little conversation.

"Where are you taking me?" She finally asked

"Away. For just a moment."

They arrived, on a winding road amid an *allée* of trees, at a small parking field. "This is Vaux-Le-Vicomte," Denys said, pointing a long arm at an exquisite small *château* not far away. "It is one of the most beautiful places in France.

"Why?"

Denys looked perplexed.

"Why do you bring me here now?"

"Because I thought you needed something wonderful to see, something French, something *classique*. You are much too involved with…." He could not finish.

"Too much involved with what?"

He took her arm. "Let's enjoy the day."

They walked down the tended path toward the *château*, built in the 1600's, with gardens laid out by Le Nôtre and Le Brun. There was a moat around the building, and fountains in a pool in the distance. Sara's spirits began to rise.

Denys led her to the stable area where highly polished *calèches* and coaches were parked, with fake horses pulling them and seated mannequins in costume. A recording of sounds of horses stamping, dogs barking as before a hunt, fanfares on trumpets, was playing throughout the stable, a live tableau.

He drove her to Barbizon, a few kilometers away, to the *Hôtellerie du Bas-Bréau,* a perfection of an inn, with doors of grilled iron, a graveled outdoor terrace, and a small fire burning in the lobby. They sat at a table in the dining room, its tablecloth covered with a pattern of deer and pheasants, dining on tiny rounds of sole on *ratatouille* with a cream sauce. They drank a red *Sancerre*, with raspberry *soufflé* for dessert. Sara's senses were newly alive. She said little, and Denys took pleasure in watching her seduction into the delights France had to offer.

They lingered over the strong *café* at the elegant table with its *sportif* cloth and decided to stroll down the main street of Barbizon, past the local artists' galleries and crafts' shops. Sara bought a pastel of a long, white picnic table in an arbor, the background teeming with masses of wild flowers. It was in a bright blue lacquer frame.

It was getting too late to return to Paris. They planned to leave in the early morning, Christmas Eve day, and drive back in leisurely fashion. Sara knew her father was still in Moscow, that she had to report to no one. Denys decided to book a room at the small *auberge* they had noticed on the side street. The *auberge* was named *L'Oignon Rouge.* Downstairs, there was a small bar where they seated themselves and each ordered a *Pernod.* For some reason unknown to herself, Sara leaned back primly and announced, "He's got a match for me."

"I can't hear you." The place was getting noisier.

"He's got a match for me," she said leaning forward.

"What is match? *allumette?*" He said laughing.

"No… no… a…well, a pairing, a man he thinks I should marry."

Denys mood sobered quickly. He sat in his chair and put his forearm across his eyes, saying nothing.

"It's a man he does business with – very rich. He owns hotels or something around the Mediterranean. He must be at least 50 years old."

Denys' lips had formed a thin line. He said nothing, then, "*Dieu*, Sara. It is not the dark ages. You're a big girl. Behave like one."

"You needn't get so upset. I haven't done anything with him."

"Who's upset," he said, sputtering. Then loudly, "What is he like, this 50 year old, rich hotel man?"

"I don't know His name's de Bouchère. He disgusts me."

Denys laughed harshly. "Doesn't that tell you something about your father? Sara, you're not a piece of goods."

"A piece of what, then?" she said defiantly.

Denys regarded her silently.

"Maybe I'm a trinket to offer de Bouchère – to bribe him with sex."

"With a remark like that, maybe you are your father's daughter." Denys' voice was filled with disgust.

Sara looked at him, then said softly, "I am my father's daughter."

"Maybe you should go to sleep with Bouchère or whatever his name is. Go ahead!" Denys exploded, jumping to his feet, nearly knocking over the chair, throwing a handful of francs on the table. He strode to the door. Sara followed quickly behind him.

L'Oignon Rouge was made of stone, a small building with a narrow staircase. Denys hastily gave the *propriétaire* a deposit in return for the key to room number four. There was only one bedroom on each of the five floors, the only *salle de bain* on the third. Denys marched angrily up the torturous stair, fumbled with the lock to their designated room, as Sara stood watching him from the landing.

"*Entrez,*" he said gruffly.

She entered the narrow room with its rough wood armoire, a bed for two on the left with a blue coverlet, and a bay window with a small loveseat built in, on which to sit and look out the leaded glass.

Sara took off her coat and laid it on a side chair. Denys was standing in the middle of the room, arms crossed over his chest, watching her. She moved to the loveseat by the bay window. It was dark outside, and there were stars above in the night sky. The stark outline of a leafless tree below was all she could see.

Denys tested the bed with a firm hand. It looked clean but none too soft, as Sara sat rigidly on her perch. He lay down silently on the bed, his face to the wall. When she heard him breathing evenly, she crept to the bed, took off her jacket and moved next to him, pressing close to the warmth of his back, all too aware of how much she needed him.

Christmas Dawn, 1979

Chapter Seventeen

Another day, another bed, this time, her father's. Sara was curled up on the puffy pillows of the raised king-size 'work-bench' (as Saul referred to it). She dozed off as she awaited his return from Moscow. The past twenty-four hours with Denys Déols had been a respite from her conflicted thoughts. The two had returned to Paris Christmas Eve, driving slowly, saying little.

He had taken her to an early dinner on the Left Bank near St. Germain, at *La Cave*, a restaurant below street level. It was a series of tiny rooms, meeting places with old brick walls, for assignations, all in a circle like she imagined a brothel to be. Over roast chicken and a beautiful sorbet, Sara's anxiety over her father returned.

"Just being back in Paris," she said wistfully

"What?" he said.

"I guess my father will return from Moscow late tonight," she said tentatively. "Tomorrow's Christmas."

"Yes? He'll be back?" Denys sounded expectant.

"Don't sound so eager," she said. "I can't help worrying if his world will be quivering yet again on the edge of disaster."

When she returned to number 17, Claus greeted her with a smirk.

He told her that Saul had called earlier. "Tell the kid I'm on my way," the German said, the guttural accent pronounced.

Now, on her father's bed, she was working on still another drawing of Saul Mammon's face. It wasn't perfect but she was proud he looked so imposing. He would like that.

Claus left the apartment to meet Saul Mammon at the Aeroflot plane at midnight in the limousine, apparently dropping off Renata at her favorite discotheque on his way to the airport. She had chosen to continue her usual round, rather than meet the plane and the man who kept her. Sara was alone at number 17. Her head nodded against the headboard.

Saul Mammon finally came through the bedroom door with Claus in tow with the suitcase. It was 2:00 AM. He did not notice his daughter on his bed. As he strode into the room, Sara heard him mumble, "Christ. This trip I really think they tried to poison me." He took off his tie, after removing the tie tack, placing both on the desk, as Claus busied himself with the suitcase. Claus put it open on its rack and cracked the French door beside the desk letting in the cool, rainy night air

"Get me some hot tea."

"You feel queasy, *Herr* Mammon?"

"*Monsieur* Mammon to you, Claus. And don't get cute with me. Berlin is just dying to know your whereabouts."

Claus left the room hurriedly, his face sullen. Her father had his back to the room, leaning over his desk, opening the dispatch case he had set upon it. Suddenly his body sagged. He turned as she rose from the bed. It was then he noticed her.

"Hey, kid," His face was pale under the swarthy skin.

"You okay?" She was alarmed.

"Sure. He straightened up, as if stung. "Why not?"

He removed his jacket in jerky motions, kicked off his shoes, and started unpacking distractedly. She sensed an unspoken flow of anxiety from him. Had he over-reached himself with the Russians? Were things closing in?

Claus appeared with a small, white pot and a Limoges cup on a tray.

"Want it?" her father asked, pointing to the tray. Sara shook her head. Claus shut the door behind him, leaving the two alone. Her father sat at the desk in his high-backed chair, his unshod feet up on the polished wood. He opened his shirt collar, pulled down the red suspenders.

"Merry Christmas," she said slowly.

"It's Christmas?" He leaned back. "You could've fooled me." He reached for his dispatch case and pulled out a dog-eared newspaper folded in half. It was Denys Déols article in <u>Le Monde</u>, dated December 20th.

"You seen this?" he said, throwing it down on the desk. She nodded. "The bastard's out to cut my balls. I should sue."

"It's mostly innuendo," Sara said hastily. "There don't seem to be many hard facts."

"So you read it. Here I give him the scoop of his life with The Red Moon so he'll take the heat off of me, and this is the thanks I get."

Her father suddenly looked at her hard. He almost did a double take. Apparently her face betrayed something for he said intuitively, "Just what do you know about this? You've been seeing this – Denys Déols?" he said suddenly, like a cat with a mouse. He smiled at her, an abrupt smile filled with violence. "You have, haven't you?"

"What?"

"Been seeing him."

"Yes." Her voice was almost inaudible.

"Why?"

"I tried to make him stop writing…this garbage."

"And?"

"He won't."

Her father started to laugh. The sound was gasping. "Of course he won't stop for a little girl like you. Did you use your feminine wiles?"

"Not exactly."

"Did they do any good? No, of course not. This asshole thinks he's got a tiger by the tail, and that he's going to make his reputation on it. Well, he does have a tiger by the tail, a cat that'll bloody him good. I'm going to cut him to ribbons. There are ways, you know. I'm perfectly capable of going for the jugular."

She stood there wavering by the bed. She had never heard him quite so frightening. His face had that look – teeth set in a ruthless clench, the nerve beneath his left eye ticking, magnified beneath his eyeglasses.

He leaned forward across the desk and pointed a finger at her. "You care about him." He said it slowly and it was no question.

When she didn't answer, he said with a sneer, "Why do you pick a loser?"

"Who says he's a loser?"

"I do. Christ, Sara, I got better men in mind for you."

"Like Manny Kiser?" she said under her breath, turning away. He did not seem to hear her.

"Like de Bouchère. Remember what I told you. You gotta put people together like equations. You and Denys Déols add up to nothing. And after all," he said, leaning back, his lips twisted, "isn't he a fanatical enemy of your old man? Christ, where's your sense of loyalty."

First, the threats, now, the guilt.

Sara crossed the room toward him slowly, ending up near the middle. She stood there, awkward. Galumphing Sara. That was her again. "The Russians," she said, eager to change the subject.

There was a long pause. "What about 'em?" He sounded evasive.

"Were they cordial? Did they...did they object to the fact you announced the opening of The Red Moon?"

"Object?" He laughed. "Of course, if you can call it that. What'd you expect? Didn't they cancel the whole damn opening? Supposed to have been today," he mused. "Yeah, you could say they were mad. But you know your old man and his silver tongue."

He stood up and picked up <u>Le Monde</u> from the desk, then threw it down impatiently. "This article didn't help. And I don't like being outsmarted. That bastard, Déols." He was pacing nervously, his limp accentuated. "Christ, I feel like I'm in a two-front war."

Depleted in his stocking feet, the left leg shorter than the right, her father looked small to her. Where always he was the center of activity, putting others into a positive swirl, at this moment the game was reversed. He was caught in an undercurrent. His guard was down this moment, this night. He was vulnerable, perhaps vulnerable enough to Sara to give the answer to what tormented her most.

"What happened?" she asked.

"In Moscow? Forget it."

"I don't mean Moscow."

He shot her a glance across the expanse of the room. The light was muted. The eagle lamp, with its two eye beams, was the only illumination.

"Between my mother and you, Daddy?"

His jaw dropped. "Anna and me? Jesus Christ, Sara. Why now? At this time of night with a load of shit on my mind!"

"I have to know." Sara turned, went over to the bed, and sat on its edge.

"Why? And what's to know? We got divorced. Period." His voice was harsh.

"Why?"

"You know marriage. No, I guess you don't." He sat again at the desk. The silence in the room extended itself. He kept tugging at his left ear. Finally he said, "I guess I was too much for her."

"You're too much for most people."

"Not for you, kid."

"You're too much for me, too. I'm not strong enough."

"Why do you add to my troubles? Are you walking out on me like your mother did, or what?"

"No, Daddy. Never. My God."

His face appeared uneven. He got up and moved again, limping She found it heartbreaking to watch him, more so to hear him, for he began to speak only to himself, as if he'd gone over it a hundred times.

"Anna...I thought sometimes she was laughing at me. Maybe because she was gentile? Anyway, it undermined me, and without my confidence, I guess I'm not a pretty sight."

He sat next to Sara on the bed, facing outward, feet on the floor, still not talking directly to her. " I used to tell her I'd get her the moon. She'd say 'No I want Venus.' I'd say, 'You are Venus. But first I'll go to God and say, Hey, God, You see there's this girl...'"

Her father's face grew shadowed. "We were at the beach house the night she left me, just when I was beginning to live rich. She hated it, said it only separated her from people. I told her we're only here on this planet for a visit, might as well lead the good life." He chuckled sadly and bowed his head in memory. "She used to say I sounded like Saul Mammon was some other person. Well, maybe he is. He's not Solly Mamminski, for sure. She called me schizo."

"Schizo? Why?" sara whispered so as not to break the spell.

"Oh, because I treat people one way and think of them in another, I guess." He paused, sighed. "Anna went upstairs that night, took you from your room in her arms, walked out the door and drove away. It was for good." He shrugged and looked at Sara at last. "At least you were a child of love, kid. But, no. I never really knew what happened."

Her father walked unsteadily to the desk and picked up the teacup, as yet untouched. He just stood there.

"What happened to all the love?" Sara asked. She could not seem to control her voice.

"I killed it, probably. I was too possessive, cut your mother off from her parents, family, friends, even from herself. She felt spied upon, mail tampered with, her conversations taped...well, you know, me and my tapes," he said, turning back to Sara with a lift of his shoulders. He went over to the black cassette case, placed beneath his desk, selected one cartridge, and shoved it hard into the stereo unit between the French doors.

Sara winced. She didn't know what to expect, but Wagner's 'Götterdammerung' issued from the loudspeakers. The dramatic music played softly as the light flickered in the room. He sat again at the desk, swinging his feet up. "I love opera," he said off-handedly, tilting his head, absorbed for a few minutes.

"One day while we were still together, she took my Thunderbird to go out from the city to the house on Long Island. Her station wagon was in the shop. She noticed how wobbly the Thunderbird drove and stopped at a gas station. All the lugs holding the four tires in place under the hubcaps had been removed. If she'd been going fast..."

"God," Sara whispered. Her dream.

He noticed the shock on her face for he said quite gently, "in my kind of operation, it happens once in a while. You should know that. Anyway, Anna was scared."

"I don't blame her."

"Neither do I. You were with her."

Again a silence deepened between the two while Sara digested this fact.

"Someday someone might really loosen your lugs," she said finally.

He roared with laughter, "Loosen my lugs. Hah! Hey kid, I'll probably outlive even you. Now let your old man get some sleep," and the vulnerability in his face closed off like a curtain coming down.

Sara went to her father at the desk. She carried his charcoal portrait. She leaned down and kissed him behind the left ear, near the awful, deadening scar. He made a little grimace, but she knew the gesture touched him because he didn't move away.

"You and mother were happy once," she said. "I'm glad you loved her. If I could only give you a little of what you had."

"Sara, you know you can't."

"Here," she said, handing him her sketch of his face.

"What's this?" He was quiet a long moment, looking at the face on the paper. "Do I really look like that?" he asked.

"I think so."

"What do you want me to do with it?"

"Keep it."

"What for?"

Sara was taken aback. "Maybe because I drew it. I just wanted you to have something…"

He laughed. "I know what I look like, and I can think of a lot of things I need more than a picture of myself. Here! You take it. So you won't forget me." He gave the sheet of paper back to her.

She stood there crushed

"Goodnight, kid."

She went to the door, crumpling the picture in her hand. As she passed the half-empty suitcase on its rack, she saw the black handle of a revolver partially covered by one of his shirts in the far corner. She stopped and picked up the ugly weapon.

"What's this?"

He didn't answer.

"Why?" she said, turning to him.

"I told you. I live in a dangerous world."

"Have you ever had to use it?"

"No," he laughed. "Hey, kid. Don't you know your old man is built like a boomerang? The harder you throw him, the faster he comes back."

She returned the gun to its place beneath the blue shirt in the suitcase. The ball of sketch paper was in her fist. She dropped it on the brown rug just inside his room as she closed the door behind her.

———

Sara could not sleep. She lay on her bed beginning another portrait of her father, in charcoal. It was kind of a love letter to him, for her own gratification, obviously not for his. He had made it painfully clear. In spite of her hurt, she had created the dimple, and a glint in the eyes where the white paper showed through, and she had caught the peculiar turn in his lips that gave his expression a 'Peck's Bad Boy' twist.

This was to have been a Christmas of such promise in Moscow, with the excitement of a great hotel opening, and the presence of her disquieting, impassioned father.

The destructive forces surrounding Saul Mammon had begun with Solly-in-the-window. Violence had been there ever since, not only in Sara's dreams. Tonight her father has revealed himself surrounded by hostile forces. Tonight, Saul Mammon had shown himself to her as he was – horribly alone and lonely. Sara had not been able to fill the gap. It was sorrowful but true. It was a lot his own fault, she thought as she drew. If he hadn't dropped out of school at 16 years old, 189 IQ and all, he might have learned to behave by rules. He might have learned to be...what? a friend?

As it was, he cut through conventional ethics and swung by the seat of his pants. He manipulated people as naturally as breathing, and lived by his favorite precepts in The Prince; 'Men must either be won over, or destroyed. Fear binds, as well or better, than love.' She remembered him telling her, 'It's no fun to play it straight.' It seemed funny at the time. Not now.

She knew the deal meant everything to him. The deal equaled an opponent, equaled confrontation, and confrontation equaled the stuff of his life. The deal evolved into a play for power at which Saul Mammon was so adept. He couldn't live without enemies. If they didn't exist, he'd have made them up.

Dimly, she heard laughter over the gentle sounds of Wagner from the direction of her father's room. He was given to insomnia and nocturnal phone calls. Probably he was relating some bad joke over the intercontinental airwaves: 'The Georgie Jessel of the Soviet Circuit,' Ephraim called him, treating the Russians to jokes and political gossip and business rumor.

Half an hour passed when suddenly Sara heard Wagner's 'Götterdammerung' turned up screechingly loud. It brought her to her feet beside the bed, hand to mouth, alert, and frightened. To hear the pounding music at full blast in the quiet of the early dawn was so bizarre. She threw on the white robe, ran down the hall, and tapped at his door. The sound was drowned out by the music.

"Daddy…" she knocked more heavily, then banged the door with her fist. "Daddy." She burst into the room, anger filling her. "It's so loud." The music was blasting. She froze. She saw her father. He was naked, draped over the high-backed desk chair like a rag doll, limbs out of joint. The French door stood ajar. The string pull of its shade hung down. It seemed to touch the body. The dangling effigy in a Brooklyn window created by young Solly Mamminski had been cut down.

She did not have to be told he was dead. She ran to him, wanting to touch him, but could only stand there, weaving. His glasses were broken pathetically beside the chair.

Suddenly a shriek filled the room. She didn't realize the ululating sound came from her because she had fainted at the look on his dead face.

December 26th, 1979

Chapter Eighteen

Sara was heavy with drugs administered by Docteur Robillion, Saul Mammon's personal physician, to dull the hysteria brought on by the grisly discovery of her father's body. Everything was fuzzy with narcotics, but memories swam up through the sedation. She was a young girl again in the house on Long Island, with her father's voice calling, "It's time to go, Sara. Get your things. You have to go back to the city." Even in her present state, tears stung her eyes, as they had so long ago. "I don't want to leave," she mumbled aloud. "You've got no choice, kid. The week-end's over."

She was aware it was over, all over. *He* was over, his last moment a fearsome one, and she thrashed convulsively, in her drugged state beneath the sheets. Christmas Day had passed for her in a miasma. "No, No, Daddy. You've been taken from me too soon. We had just begun," she murmured, overcome by loss, made excruciating because she'd had him so briefly.

Near dusk, she became conscious of the face of Denys Déols, the tousled dark hair, the dark eyes. He was bending over her, looking down at her. Behind him, she began to see the beige and cream room, hear soft voices in the distance and then his words.

"I'm here, Sara."

"Oh Denys We had just..." she turned her head to the pillow. "It's true then, isn't it?" She whispered. "I didn't dream it, did I? He's dead isn't he?"

"Yes."

"What am I to do? I can't live without him."

"This you must learn to do, live without."

She wept softly.

"I'm so sorry you were the one to find him," he said.

"Better me than anyone else."

Manny Kiser hovered into view, and she turned her head until he went away. She slept again.

When she awoke it was deep night. There was a small lamp lighted next to the door of her bedroom. She was alone. She managed to rise to her feet in the dimness and put on the white robe.

She walked weakly down the red-carpeted hall. Suddenly, her eyes saw clearly the objects she passed in detail, as if in slow motion. She studied the porcelain figurines of animals and birds of prey that adorned the walls of the long corridor. She passed photographs of her father with Lyndon Johnson and Jimmy Carter.

She paused at a teak plaque with bronze letters mounted on the paneling. She had never noticed it before. It was from the Italian government to SAUL MAMMON in honor of his organizing THE FREEDOM TRAIN, dated 1946. The train had traveled the length of the United States, gathering railroad cars full of food for the Italian people decimated by World War II.

THE FREEDOM TRAIN. She touched the plaque. It was testimony to a certain decency of her dead father. He had had his moments.

She reached the brown bedroom. There was a police notification in French posted on the door. It was sealed by a wire stretching across the crack. She managed to undo this with the metal nail file in the pocket of her robe, delicately, so she could reattach it on her way out. Sara stood in the open doorway. The room looked exactly as it had when she had been with him last night, first, so alive, and later, when she found him dead. The body was gone but a livid bloodstain on the back of the desk chair seemed to beckon. The French door was standing open as it had been earlier. She looked closely at the string of the shade that so looked to her like doctor's gauze suspended from a hanger in an old Brooklyn window.

The brain protects itself to some extent, particularly with the help of potions from a Docteur Robillon, but Sara was unprepared for the impact of the little things she saw in the intimacy of his bedroom. 'Götterdammerung' was still in the tape deck, switched off. <u>Le Monde</u> was on the desk next to his dispatch case where he had thrown it, his striped tie and tie tack lying beside it. The small, black tape recorder and cassette carrying case were on the floor beneath the desk.

She went over to the bed. It was rumpled with the impress of his body, the pillows in disarray; the little things, his little things, awaiting his hand; the telephone silent in its cradle with its eight buttons unlit, and next to it, a pile of papers and file folders. And then she saw, on top of the pile, her crumpled picture of his face, the one she had dropped on the floor. It had been smoothed out and in his own hand, he had written: 'Saul Mammon, by his beloved daughter, December 25th, 1979.' Sara burst into tears.

She stood without moving in the middle of the room. He had saved it!

As she started to leave, she passed the suitcase still open on its rack, half-unpacked, just as it had been earlier that night. As she walked by, she looked for the handle of the revolver under his blue shirt. The shirt was there. The gun was gone.

Next morning, sunlight entered Sara's bedroom through the blinds, as she awoke aching in her bed to the sound of men talking.

"You here again?" It was Manny Kiser's voice.

"That's right," said Déols.

"You shouldn't have come yesterday. You shouldn't be here today. Get out."

She roused up on the pillows. "Wait. I want him here, Manny."

"The man who trashed your father?"

"I want him here," she repeated.

Manny mumbled something that sounded suspiciously like 'serpent's tooth,' and slid away, closing the door behind him.

Denys sat down in the bedside chair. A long moment passed. "He thinks we're lovers," he said.

She didn't answer.

"It bothers you?"

She nodded.

Then he said softly, "The violent loss of a father is always a terrible blow to the psyche of a loving daughter, but it's devastating if she's got a bad conscious. Do you have a bad conscience?"

She nodded again.

"About me?"

Another nod.

"Do you want me to leave?"

Sara shook her head vigorously. "Tell me what happened?" she said.

"You're sure you're ready?"

"Yes."

Denys told her how Claus had come on the run from the servants' quarters when he first heard her cry, all on one note. Claus had said the scream was the same sound that mourning Arab women made on mountaintops in North Africa. Claus had first heard that eerie wail as a 17-year-old soldier in Algiers during World War II.

In her father's bedroom, Sara had been lying on the floor beside the desk chair over which her father's body was incongruously draped. Claus checked her pulse before going to Saul Mammon's body. Bloodstains from the mouth had spread on the fabric of the chair. He almost touched the throat, but leaned down instead near the mouth, seeking a sign of breath. There was none. He then moved to the stereo, clicking off Wagner, still at full decibel, before going to the telephone and calling the Prefecture of Police, 16th Arrondissement.

Denys told this matter-of-factly, as if he were reading from his notebook. He was. Sara listened, eyes closed. He told her the police, Docteur Robillon, and the coroner had determined her father had suffered a massive coronary. Paris Soir, The New York Times, and The Washington Post, as well as his own news editor at Le Monde, had termed it cardiac arrest. It was the official line from the American Embassy in Paris.

As he recited this list of media pronouncements, Sara began shaking her head.

"Cardiac arrest? No."

"You doubt it?"

Her mouth twisted. "You didn't see the look on his face. There was a revolver in his suitcase when I was with him earlier in the evening. When I went into his room later last night…after…" she faltered. "The gun was gone."

"Maybe the police took it."

"Or the killer," she said. "It was murder. I know it."

"All the papers…"

"DamnDéols. Do you believe everything you read in the newspapers? Get me copies."

"Even the American Embassy. They're making noises."

"A cover–up," she choked.

"That's a serious accusation."

"Murder is a serious crime. A cover-up. I know it."

"Well, you better not say that to anyone but me."

"Why?"

"They won't believe you. They'll think you're crazy. They'll rationalize it away." He arose from the chair and leaned over her. "But I happen to think you're right,"he whispered. "I'll bring those newspapers," and he left abruptly.

December 27th, 1979

Chapter Nineteen

Sara was still shaky with sedatives as she inspected the masses of flowers, reading through hazy eyes, the cards on the wreaths and arrangements. It was four o'clock in the afternoon. The bank of flowers was spread across one of the hotel tables of the Coeur d'Or in the lavish reception room set to shelter the Memorial Service for Saul Mammon.

One elaborate bouquet had a heavily engraved card with an Athens address that read simply, 'Christina,' another, just 'Roone,' another Yuri Novikov, USSR Committee for Science and Tecnology.' Another card with a huge potted plant had 'Senator' (name crossed out) and the one word 'Scoop' in longhead beneath, and there was a second senatorial card with 'Ted' scribbled on it. These represented only a handful from the mountains of flowers.

The perfume from the bower filled the room. She glanced around the premises. In her daze, it reminded her of a sitting-room in a whorehouse, or what she supposed one would look like, with its red velvet curtains at the three windows overlooking Avenue George V, and red wallpaper that shimmered on the walls, and that terrible sweet smell.

There was an oak table in the corner holding a tray of liquor and one of *hors d'oeuvres,* Sara guessed to be compliments of the hotel management. Apparently, they didn't know that food is not generally served at Jewish funerals, much less alcohol. To the Coeur d'Or, it was just another catered affair.

The young American Rabbi stood before the fireplace. He looked uncomfortable and not very religious, dressed in street clothes with a checkered jacket. He had a scraggly, thin moustache. Were it not for the yarmulke on his head, she imagined he looked like one of the whorehouse customers, awaiting his turn.

An astonishingly small number of people were paying their respects to the deceased: Manny (in yarmulke), Ephraim (bare-headed), Claus (in shiny blue suit). Where was Renata? Sara had not seen her, nor heard from her, since the fatal night. Was she somewhere in a state of hysteria? After all, she just lost her meal ticket, Sara thought unkindly.

A pair of anonymous men in gray suits with black armbands and crew cuts (American Embassy?) stood near the windows. One of them sported a heavy gold class ring. She noticed he also wore yellow socks. Near the open double doors of the entry, a man in a musty brown suit with soup spots on the lapel, leaned against the doorjamb, an obvious policeman, an obvious Frenchman. In the corner stood the rumpled Denys Déols. He seemed remote to her until their glances entangled intensely.

Suddenly, there was her mother, a solitary figure behind the flowers in a dark coat her blond head very still, the features composed.

Sara rushed to her and threw her arms around her. The two women, mother and daughter, bent to one another in sorrow.

"You came," Sara said, voice choked.

"How could I not? You look white as a ghost. Are you all right?" She nodded.

"I'm so sorry it had to be you," Anna said, taking Sara's hands in her own, "So very sorry, darling."

A terrible sound of the double doors slamming shut filled the reception room. Renata had entered in a black hat and heavy veil. Her eyes glittered behind the netting, bespeaking an extra snort of coke or two.

She leaned back dramatically against the doors in her all black outfit with tight pants and shiny boots. Her arms were spread out at her sides. She looked like a black widow spider, splayed there against the door, and from a distance, she appeared bizarre and unsavory.

"I stop proceedings. There will be no ceremony," Renata shouted in a thick voice.

Sara glanced at Denys. He had pricked up his ears.

"Come on, Renata." Manny started toward her.

"You," she screamed at him. "You are just who I wish to see. What about my settlement?"

"Renata, this is not the time and place, " Manny muttered.

"I want to know my settlement."

"Christ, you weren't even married to him. Come on." He went to her and tried to take her arm.

She pulled away angrily and waved a hand toward the bank of flowers and the food and drink. "This is all fake, all fake, like everything else about Saul Mammon. Including his death. There's something fishy there." (She pronounced it 'feeshy.') "All swept – how do you say – under rug." Her face shone with excitement behind the dusky veil.

The people in the red room were mesmerized by the performance.

"Cover-up!" Screeched Renata.

Sara had used the phrase herself. She turned quickly to find Denys. He was directly behind her and put a hand under her elbow.

"You're crazy," muttered the larger of the Bobbsy twins from the Embassy. "It was a heart attack."

"Then why broken larynx?" yelled back Renata.

Sara turned to Denys, aghast.

"Yes," said the journalist. "A hairline crack." Sara had been so sedated, the fact that her father had had a broken larynx when he died escaped her. Renata had begun to sob. Tears were dripping into the veil so it stuck to her face. The two men in gray moved beside Renata, one at each arm.

"Come now, Miss," the one with the gleaming ring said, firmly gripping her arm with one hand and opening the double doors with the other. Renata disappeared, lifted from the ground by the two Embassy officials. As the doors closed behind her, Sara caught a glimpse of the man in the brown suit approaching the threesome in the hall. The German woman was outnumbered. Sara could hear her loudly cursing in her native tongue all the way into the lobby.

The incident did not help the mood of the Memorial Service. The Rabbi cleared his throat. He looked sick with embarrassment. He was a tweedy, earnest sort who found himself, as the saying goes, in the wrong pew. He had the distasteful duty to have to eulogize someone in death he had never known, and Saul Mammon surely wouldn't have entered this particular fellow's synagogue. The small group gathered in desultory fashion before the Rabbi, as Manny made a gesture of disgust toward the food.

"Get rid of that stuff," he hissed to Claus. As they moved to confront the Rabbi with their backs to the German chauffeur, out of the corner of her eye, Sara saw Claus look around wildly, loaded tray of liquor in hand. He shoved it under the table, followed by the food platters.

The Rabbi droned on in a nasal American accent. Sara stood shoulder to shoulder with her mother. Anna's face revealed nothing. Denys was back in his corner. It was a mercifully short ceremony. The Rabbi finished intoning the Kaddish in Hebrew with relief. When Sara looked at her mother again, she saw her eyes had filled with tears, but they did not spill over.

Everyone moved heavily. The doors were opened, the food and drink remained under the table, and the cluster of people filed out. Sara saw that the French policeman in the brown suit had not returned to his post, nor had the two Embassy men. At the top of the hall, everyone, including Déols, was met by a barrage of press people. In flying-wedge formation, the group skittered through their grasp. One male and one female journalist managed to collar Manny and Ephraim.

"What was Saul Mammon really like?" the woman said aggressively in a high breathy voice.

"The best businessman in the world," replied Ephraim, pushing through.

"Yeah," echoed Manny. Then under his breath, he added, "taken out of the play too fucking soon."

Through the commotion around her, Sara heard one male reporter ask, "Who's the brunette with the big eyes?"

"Oh, that's Mammon's kid."

"Yeah?" The reporter sound surprised. "Mammon had a kid?" As the press was left in their wake, Sara heard Manny say to Ephraim, "Saul measured his own coffin years ago," and they were through the lobby and out in the dusk of the street.

Chapter Twenty

Déols left Sara with her mother under the red-canopied entrance of the Coeur d'Or. Thank God Anna was there, Sara thought. The two women turned the corner of avenue George V, and started to walk slowly up the Champs-Elysées toward the Étoile in the gathering night. There was a fine drizzle.

"Where are you staying?" She asked Anna.

"At the Hotel Bellegarde on the Left Bank. You know, lots of velvet walls and ornate tiny furniture."

"When do you go back to New York?"

"Tomorrow."

"So soon. You won't stay longer?"

"If you want me to," her mother replied, pausing on the pavement.

"No, It's not necessary…but…" They were standing in front of the famous *Fouquet's* restaurant. Sara grabbed her mother's gloved hand, drawing her into the entrance.

"Please," she said. "It seems such a long time, you know, since we were together. Please stay. Talk to me for a while this evening."

"Of course," Anna replied, smiling. "But it only seems long. We had dinner the night before you left. It's just that so much has happened."

They found a booth underneath a wooden-framed mirror that stretched the length of the sidewall and ordered a carafe of red wine from the waiter in his long white apron. The place was almost empty.

Only a pair of old men conversed with animation at a corner table in the rear over their *Pernods*, speaking in rapid French, as the *propriétaire* behind the bar with its brass fittings, threw in florid comments.

The two women awaited the wine to arrive in silence. Anna removed her gloves. "I'll stay if you want. I'll stay in Paris."

"No." Sara shook her head.

"You shouldn't remain, Sara."

"I must find out the truth."

"Don't do this to yourself." Echoes of her father.

"It was murder," Sara said softly.

"No. No." Anna shook her head vigorously. She took a long sip of wine. "And even if it were, better let it rest. Leave it alone."

"I can't."

Anna sighed. "I always knew it was important for you to come to Paris with Saul. He was never in one place long enough for you to really know what he was all about," she said.

"I feel I know even less about him than when I first came, two weeks ago. Is that all it's been?" Sara suddenly exploded. "Two weeks. More like a lifetime. Or a death time. From the second the Concorde lifted off, I felt I was on a great voyage of discovery that suddenly turned garish and weird and very, very bumpy."

Anna touched her hand. "It was more like being aboard the 'Titanic'."

"Every question I had was met with a question," Sara went on. "Even though I think he really tried to give himself to me emotionally."

"He couldn't, darling. Don't you understand? Your father was hollow inside. There was an emotional vacuum. It was a form of illness."

Sara was sniveling into a Kleenex. "I'm sorry," she said, her voice muffled. She waved the white tissue high in the air. "He treated people like this," she said, balling the Kleenex, flinging the offending stuff on the black and white tile floor of *Fouquet's*. The waiter glanced at her across the room with a raised eyebrow.

Her mother removed her coat. Beneath it, she wore a silk dress the color of sea shells. She was a pole apart from the outrageous Renata in her orange caftan and fringed suede, the two sides of Saul Mammon incarnate.

"Don't be upset Sara. Have some wine. You know your father."

"No I don't. I only know he was the kind of man who ate people for breakfast."

"Oh now. You're right, but…I remember his mother asking me… it was just before we were married, 'aren't you afraid?' I thought it a bit peculiar," Anna said ruefully

"What did she mean?"

"That he gave reason to be afraid. That *she* was."

Suddenly angry, Sara blurted, "For God's sake, how did it even start, you and he?"

"We met on a blind date. You know his charm," Anna said, raising her chin and looking off into some distant place. She leaned against the old leather of the banquette. "You know how vital he was, how full of life."

"But what happened between you?" Sara interjected.

"He was a boy-man with a terrible dark side, a side that no one could see at first. Somehow he seemed to think I was looking down on him, feeling superior or something."

"Did you?"

"No, of course not. In the beginning, I worshipped him." Anna's face was pale. She shook her head "Later, I began to feel like a ghost in his life, not necessary to him as he played the big man. I was only a trophy on his arm, someone to pave the way to social circles, even to do some of his dirty work. I found I was – I don't know – becoming like him in a way – unscrupulous. He seemed to have devoured me – my integrity – the real me. I didn't like myself any more. I had to leave." Anna's voice drifted off.

Sara sat spellbound.

Then, her mother continued, her voice deepening, "Saul had a lot of enemies. I knew someone was out to kill him. Even then. I thought they might kill me too   and you! I was scared." She paused. "I'll never forget those final moments before I left him." Anna shook her head, as if to free herself of the memory. "Ever since, I've been trying to live my life as if he'd never been a part of it – but you know that's impossible." She smiled pensively at her daughter.

"And what about me?"

"Oh, darling, you were our love child."

Sara visualized her father and mother together, as they had been when she was little, the way the sparks flew between them, and how her mother was full of zest and energy. Those early days on Long Island with the sand dunes to run upon and the labrador puppies and the gracious house with its open veranda, overlooking an inlet surrounded by tall reeds that hid the swans and their cygnets, that used to occasionally rush up the lawn, scaring the small girl – those early days were gone so quickly.

"He was the most jealous person I ever met," Anna was saying, her body stiffening. "Jealous of everybody, even jealous of the time I spent with you, but it's lucky you were a girl. A son would have threatened him on every level. He would have brutalized a boy in whatever manner he chose."

"And you left him." Sara's tone was matter-of-fact.

Anna looked startled. "I was chattel…goods…loving is not a business deal, Sara." And she looked at her daughter straight in the eye.

"He was my father. I worry. I still worry even though he's gone."

"You mustn't anymore. You can't. It's bad for you. Besides, darling," Anna said in a firmer tone, "if you must know, I didn't like being married to a tape recorder. Have you ever heard yourself played back on that bloody little machine?"

"Me?"

"What makes you think you'd be exempt?"

Sara's mouth dropped.

Anna rose, pulling her coat about her. She put some francs on the table.

"Did it ever occur to you, it might have been partly your fault too?" Sara said too boldly, looking up at her.

Anna flushed. "Yes. I'm sure it was my fault, too. Sometimes, I could be pretty cold, pretty unkind…even bitchy, I know it," her mother responded. "Come on. It's time to go."

They walked in silence up the Champs-Elysées. Near *Le Drug Store*, they passed a kiosk with magazines, journals, periodicals laid out in colorful rows. Both of them involuntarily slowed their steps, scanning the headlines of newspapers, seeking God knows what, an announcement of Saul Mammon's demise? But there was none.

Instead, they were met with the blazing headline of the Soviet invasion of Afghanistan in large letters on the front page of every newspaper on display. Sara noticed the name of Yuri Novikov, prominent at the top of the article in <u>The International Herald Tribune</u>. It was Novikov who had ordered the violation of the Afghan border with hundreds of planes, helicopters, thousands of men. Novikov had commanded a superior violence, and he had been her father's mighty good friend in the Kremlin. Would Novikov have bothered with the murder of one man? Or could Saul Mammon have had something to do with the Russian buildup of arms on the Afghan border? Sara stumbled at this horrifying speculation. The U.S. microchips? What had been on them?

She shivered as they passed the kiosk and crossed the avenue. As the two walked the last steps to the entrance of number 17, Sara looked up over the courtyard wall to his bedroom balcony. It was dark there, no light behind the French doors that led inside to the brown room. She shivered again.

The two women stood face to face. "Do you want to come up?" Sara asked, her voice trembling.

Anna shook her head, then put her arms around her daughter and held her close. There was an unspoken apology in the embrace.

"It's all right," Sara murmured. "I'm all right" Then, "He never got over you, you know. You did love him once, didn't you?"

Anna looked down, then, lifted eyes that glistened more brightly than the wet pavement at their feet. "Yes, Sara, I did. Oh yes." She paused. "The only reason he never got over me was because no one left Saul Mammon. No one!"

Sara took her mother's hand. "I hope he loved me. I always wondered."

"Of course he did. You were...are...what's yet to come...the future! You know he did, dear girl, but please, leave Paris," Anna said, her voice pleading.

"I must stay." Sara's quest had taken on new import.

They looked at each other for a long moment, and then Anna whispered into the damp night, "Just love people, Sara. And love him, even after he's gone."

"Do you?"

Anna nodded, and in her dark coat and light hair, Sara saw her mother move silently up the street toward the glittering Arc de Triomphe. She watched until Anna disappeared into the night, then turned, and steeled herself against entering the apartment, a residence now transformed to one of pain, with that miserable woman inside. Renata! How could he? Sara thought, glancing back toward the Étoile where the silhouette of her mother seemed to linger in the mist.

Mercifully the apartment was empty.

December 28, 1979

Chapter Twenty-One

"Saul Mammon, American financier, dead in his apartment on avenue Foch." It was a teletype printout in bleak letters, dated Paris, December 25th, 1979. A friend of Denys Déols had filched it from the American Embassy newsroom.

Sara stared at it on top of the broad table in her father's office conference room. It looked so small and insignificant lying there, just a strip of white paper with little black markings to record the dreadful moment. Next to it lay a copy of the <u>New York Daily News</u> also dated Christmas Day. The headline read, "Saul Mammon Dead in Paris --- U.S. Entrepreneur's Soviet Ties."

Beside that lay the front page of the Financial Section of the <u>New York Times</u>, dated December 26, 1979. The headline was three columns wide: "Saul Mammon's Death Reveals Complex Deals," and the top of the story began:

> "Saul Mammon, a mysterious and controversial entrepreneur who was one of the leading businessmen in East-West trade, died in his Paris apartment yesterday at the age of 60."

Next to the story was a graph of his business activities: holding companies, joint ventures, dummy corporations. Solly Mamminski's death had not gone unnoticed.

Spread out upon the table, there were also issues of Paris Soir, The International Herald Tribune, Le Figaro, all with similar stories, all evincing a certain confusion about Saul Mammon's life and career, all showing no confusion at all as to the cause of his death: cardiac arrest. All but one, that is. Le Monde. In his article, Deny Déols had left a question mark. "Heart attack, or murder?"

In a navy blue suit, Sara pored over the newspapers. She was standing, leaning with elbows on the table, devouring the printed word, her hips thrust back unconsciously and the curve of her spine elongated. She didn't mean to be provocative, but the man with the rough, black, hair standing next to her seemed to grow increasingly nervous.

"You're the only one," she said, surprised by his presence, as she studied the pages before her, unexpectedly enjoying her effect on him.

"Only a hint, really. Only a question."

"But you're the only one."

"Here, look at this," he said, pointing to the middle of the article in L'Evenment.

> "The American Embassy, through the American Ambassador, has announced that the French coroner found massive heart lesions. He pronounced conclusively the cause of death as cardiac arrest. 'As Saul Mammon died alone in his own bedroom, there is no evidence of foul play,' said the Embassy spokesman."

"That's the official word," said Denys.

"A cover-up!" Sara blurted out. "And the New York papers probably bought it too."

"Not just New York. It's all over – the London papers, Rome…"

"Moscow?"

"I don't know."

"But not you," she said softly. "Not Le Monde."

"I wrote all I know of that night – the French door ajar, the broken larynx, the blood on the chair. I'm sorry," he said when he saw her wince.

"Why do they cover it up?" she burst out. "They don't even allow the possibility of a crime."

Denys shrugged. "Maybe they don't know. We'll have to do some serious digging. I'm not going to let this pass."

"Nor am I," she said, straightening up and looking into his eyes. They stood there, barely touching, when Manny Kiser came into the conference room. He wore a coat of cashmere that seemed several sizes too large for him. He stopped when he saw them standing close.

"Christ. Not you again."

"I'm afraid so," Denys said easily, still lost in Sara's eyes.

"And what is all this?" Manny replied, picking up the New York Times.

"Self-evident, Monsieur Kiser."

Manny spotted the copy of Le Monde on the table. He pointed to it. "How come you're the only one who called it murder?" the lawyer said aggressively.

"I didn't say it was murder. I just suggested there might be more of a mystery than anyone seems to admit."

"Well, kill that idea. It was a heart attack, pure and simple."

"Not so pure. Not so simple," Sara interjected.

"I'm not saying Saul Mammon mightn't have deserved it," Manny said with a grimace.

"Why do you say that?" Denys asked

"You suggest it's murder, Déols. People do not get murdered usually unless they're capable of the same."

"Yes?" Déols eyes were bright with interest.

"I think it's best you leave," Manny said abruptly. "I have certain financial questions to discuss with the heir here. It's private."

She looked at the tall Frenchman beseechingly. He slowly shook his head and spoke to her above the top of the lawyer's skull. "It's best I go," he said and he left quickly.

"Well, my dear, is it serious?" Manny asked sarcastically with a jerk of his thumb in the direction of Denys Déols' exit.

"I thought you had business to discuss with me."

Manny sat at the head of the long table his coat dragging on the floor. "Saul Mammon lived like a rich man. He died a pauper."

Sara swallowed hard. "The apartment?"

"Month to month lease. Same with the office."

"The yacht?"

"Owned by three corporations, in none of which he owned a controlling interest. Of course, Renata's convinced he secreted money in many countries and companies. She may be right. She's determined to track down his assets." Manny laughed. "It shows how Saul conned her. God's little joke on people like Renata is that they're doomed to believe others, like Saul, aren't as tricky as they are," he said smugly.

"Are you referring to yourself too, Manny?"

"I'm sure he had secret accounts, but Saul was the only one who knew where to find them, and if I can't find them, do you really think Renata can? All that gold stockpiled and only Saul knew where."

He glared at her.

"How was he able to live in such opulence?"

"Your father outdistanced his creditors. That's all, though I must say the fabric of his life had grown a little threadbare." He looked down his nose.

"What creditors?" Sara was truly shocked, and sank into the nearest executive chair.

"Oh, his tailor in London, his shoemaker in Italy, the boatyard in the South of France. You name it." He chuckled with a kind of satisfaction she found revolting. "Oh and don't forget the banks. Mustn't forget them. Saul knew a great secret. If you owe enough money, there is nothing your bankers can do except lend you more.

It requires charm and chutzpah. Saul had both. He would go to a financier about to call a loan and walk out with twice as much for a new project."

"I don't believe you."

"The financier would sit there and shake his head and say to himself, 'what happened?'" said Manny with another laugh. "Oh, I've seen Saul perform. In those sanctified offices, I often watched his exercise in democratic 'taking,' from the biggest banks to the smallest neighbors. It didn't matter to Saul which."

"You certainly don't sound like my father's friend, Manny." He looked at her slyly from under his brow. "Which are you?" she said.

"Which what?"

"Enemy or stooge?"

Manny laughed uneasily. "You're beginning to sound like him."

"I'm myself," she said, but his words shook her. "Is there a will?"

"Renata claims she has a handwritten piece of paper promising the little German cunt a fortune. The problem is, other than the fact that there is no fortune, it was written on an airplane. That makes the paper illegal. No domicile. Did you know that? I can assure you, your father did know. By the way, I leave for New York tonight."

"You're leaving this mess?"

"What mess?"

"His death," she cried out. "There are so many unanswered questions."

"Like what?"

"Oh, I don't know. Like…Michelson Frères…the Olympic Gold Coin sets…what about them?"

"Maybe later – at a later date. But there are bills to pay NOW." Manny stood up. "However, you needn't worry about those at the moment. He left some cash," he said, his face twisted. "Your father believed in fresh C-notes."

He reached in his briefcase and pulled out several stacks of hundred dollar bills with the bank wrappers still around each. He put them on the conference table in front of her. "Here. You might need this."

Sara was dumbfounded.

"He kept money in desk drawers, glove compartments. Even in his toilet case." Manny looked down at her. "But cash won't pay his enormous debts. Overall, we'll probably declare bankruptcy - undoubtedly the best route. What a tangle! His hidden accounts are just that. Buried. Lost. If we do declare bankruptcy and can't establish domicile, Saul Mammon could be buried in the French equivalent of Potter's Field."

"What are you saying?"

"We may have to."

"Potter's Field. Never. My father?" She was trembling uncontrollably.

"It may have to be, kiddie. Now take it easy. You really are coming apart."

Manny was still in his oversized coat, standing there with a strange expression on his face. "Let me give you a piece of advice. Get off this murder kick, you and your friend Déols. I advise you, Sara, for your own good, leave it lay. You might be taking on the whole U.S. Government and the Russians as well." There was such a threat in his voice, her trembling increased.

"You can't leave." She heard her own voice from a distance. They were alone in the office. When he put his hand out to touch her, she drew back violently.

"Oh, I thought for a moment your desire to have me stay might have been an invitation," he said with a snarl, and with that he angrily left the room, drowned in his coat, reddish hair stiff on his head.

Chapter Twenty-Two

Ephraim found her in the conference room. He sat down heavily beside her. "Are you okay, Sara?" he asked gently. She shook her head.

After several moments he ventured, "it's like Saul's not really gone. He's just on another trip."

"He is on another trip, Ephraim," she said bitterly. The big Israeli watched her closely, concerned.

There was a long silence. Then he said, "I don't mean to hurt you more, but there were times I wished him dead. Does that shock you?"

"Suddenly he is dead. Does that shock you?"

"I don't know how to feel," he sighed. "Right now, I'm considering going home. Saul's dead. He doesn't need me anymore, and, frankly, it's a relief."

Sara was chilled because she had thought Ephraim was genuinely fond of her father. She decided at that moment if Saul Mammon confounded his enemies, he also confounded his friends.

"It never ceases to amaze me how we Jews can fight each other to death one day and turn around and work together on the next, if it's profitable, and working with Saul was very profitable indeed."

"If you felt that way about him, why'd you stay associated with him? Just profit?" she erupted, rising and pacing around the table.

'Ah, ah Sara. I loved Saul Mammon. I found him irresistible. And he was a lesson for all of us. He had the grace to occasionally make a fool of himself."

"What do you mean?" she said angrily.

"I remember when he got the first yacht...through corporations, of course. He had to buy a Captain's hat, too. Saul said, 'Look. I'm a Captain,' as he popped the cap on his head. I said, 'My God, man. By me you're a Captain. By you, you're a Captain. But by a Captain, you're not a Captain.'" Ephraim's eyes were shining with amusement. "How Saul laughed. That's what I mean, Sara. He knew when he was playing the fool. And he had chutzpah. My God he had it," said Ephraim, slapping his knee. "Captain Mammon, King of the Sea! How he loved that first boat, 'Mammon's Desire.' I remember the night in August when she blew..."

"You were there?" Sara asked, sitting in the chair beside him.

Ephraim nodded, his face lost in memory.

"I never saw anything like it."

"The explosion?"

"No, not just the explosion. Saul's *sangfroid.*" Ephraim shook his head.

"We had gone up to the *Coeur d'Or* for dinner. Saul had gotten a sudden yen for a particular chicken dish they make. The restaurant is on the side of the hill overlooking the harbor. We could see 'Mammon's Desire' riding proudly at anchor quayside below. She looked beautiful, all lit up. Saul was putting her in dry dock for the winter the next day. He'd just had her rewired. Suddenly, the damn thing exploded in flames with a great roar. There was consternation in the restaurant. Even the chef came running from the kitchen. Saul just sat there lapping up the chicken in champagne sauce. 'My God, Saul, we were supposed to have dined aboard tonight,' I said to him. He just looked at me. Everyone in the place was watching him. They all knew it was his boat, the guy with the yachting cap on the back of his head, busily cleaning his plate. 'Christ Saul,' I said to him. 'How can you just sit there?' 'Why should I watch the death throes?' he said. 'It's only a boat. Like a woman, there'll always be another.'"

Sara was caught up in Ephraim's words. "Go on," she whispered.

"That boat…it was his favorite toy. Someone didn't want him to have it. Someone didn't want him at all."

"Are you saying…? "The thought, the possibility of the yacht exploding on purpose sickened her.

Ephraim shrugged. "It was no accident, Sara. ' Mammon's Desire' was in perfect condition."

There was a long silence. She sat there, numb beyond reason, before Ephraim continued. "There was a gentleman in the restaurant that night, kind of classy, in a blue blazer, sitting alone on the far side. He came over to our table and said, very British, 'Excuse me, sir, is that your ship down there in the harbor?' 'It was,' said Saul. 'Permit me to introduce myself. I'm James Chapin, London… Chapin-Euro-Tel Limited, the hotel syndicate? We own hotels at Heathrow, at Orly, the Coeur d'Or on Avenue George Cinq, with a branch of this very restaurant in the middle of its wine cellar.' Saul pushed his cap even farther back on his head, as Chapin said, ' I just wanted to remark that anyone who has the cool to sit and sup as his yacht is being blown sky high has got to come and work for me.' And Saul came back with, 'Well, sit right down Jim. Have a liqueur.' The honeymoon was on."

"That's how he got into the hotel business?"

"You bet. The deal for The Red Moon? That was done with Chapin, but in the process of building the hotel in Moscow, there was a falling out between the two, as always with Saul's partners."

"Except you, Ephraim," she said softly.

"'Course, Saul continued to use Chapin's name to cinch other deals. Chapin was furious. He cut his losses, leaving Saul alone on The Red Moon, with the Soviet Government of course, and Michelson Frères as underwriter, the same three that were launching the Olympic franchises. But that evening in August, all was sweetness between them, like falling in love. People often did that with Saul. I remember that night on the hill. I walked out of the restaurant ahead of the two of them, watched them shake hands. Then, Saul stood there alone for a moment. He took off his yachting cap and scrunched it together and threw it to the stones of the terrace floor amid the bird droppings. I went over to him. He said, 'There'll be another boat, Ephraim. I promise you,' but his voice was funny. He never showed to anyone what the loss of 'Mammon's Desire' had really cost him."

"Except maybe to you," she said.

"I loved the bastard," Ephraim said, his voice low and uneven.

"So did I," she said and started to cry.

"Now, now," he said, patting her hand. "Anything I can do to help, you know I will. He'd want me to. Besides, you're special. You're Anna's daughter, too."

She smiled tentatively at him. Then, "Manny says we're bankrupt."

"Probably."

"Manny said…he said…Daddy might have to be buried in the French version of Potter's Field."

"That Manny is very smart, but he's hardly a diplomat," Ephraim said, rising. "Don't worry. I promise you, it will not be Potter's Field for Saul. I can't guarantee he'll be…that his body will be returned to the States, but I do promise you no Potter's Field. Maybe Père Lachaise, if I can swing it."

"How?"

"I have connections."

He sat beside her. "Please, my dear, wipe your tears. I'll do whatever I can."

"What happened the night he died, Ephraim?"

He just looked at her.

"Do you believe it was just a heart attack?"

"I really wish you wouldn't ask me this."

"I have to know. I deserve to know," she said imploringly.

Ephraim cast his eyes to heaven. He gave a sad little laugh. The metal incisors gleamed. He shook his bear head from side to side, anything to avoid answering, then turned and looked at her directly.

"Yes. You of all people have a right to the truth. Of course it wasn't just a heart attack."

Sara could hardly breathe. "Ephraim...please..."

"There is a form of assassination," he started slowly. "For it was that, my dear. It is called by professionals, 'The Bulgarian Method.'" He looked at her tear-stained face with concern. She nodded for him to go on.

"The perpetrator uses an undetectable gas over the nose. First he cracks the larynx with a karate chop and the poisonous gas is sucked into the lungs. It stops the heart...takes seconds... It's been used frequently in Europe since the war."

Sara's eyes must have grown round and bright with horror for Ephraim stopped cold. "I'm so sorry, my dear," he said, "but your father was dealing for the highest stakes, amongst the most venal people and governments in a maze of skullduggery. It had to happen."

"But how? How could someone get in his bedroom? I was right down the hall."

"It's very easy to get to the balcony over the courtyard. Any second-story man could do it. Saul always kept the French doors ajar at night."

"Do you think it might have been a person he knew?"

"Certainly the man who ordered it."

"Novikov?"

He shook his head.

"James Chapin?"

Again he shook his head.

"Closer to home? Renata? Manny? Herman Tyson?" she said, wildly.

"No...no."

"Who then, for God's sakes?"

"I believe it was The Company," was his low reply.

She threw up her hands. "What company? He worked for dozens," she said with irritation.

"*THE* Company." He paused while Sara continued to fume. "The CIA."

She looked at Ephraim with disbelief. "The American CIA?"

"Is there any other?"

"His own countrymen?"

"Saul had no country. He just dipped into the States. You know that."

"Oh, Ephraim, why? Why?" She was now crying full out.

"Saul had gotten dangerous to them. They knew he was dealing both sides."

"I don't believe it."

"I was with him on some of it. I hate to admit it. He had become an admitted agent of the Soviets. He told me."

"What?" She blanched. "But...there are double-agents. They don't get killed."

"He was a renegade. It had to happen. If The Company hadn't done it, the KGB would have."

"So it was the KGB," she said, grabbing at this. It was so much more acceptable to her.

"No. I don't think so. Surely they were growing suspicious. Saul had me devise a system to inflate expenses and conceal profits on the false flag operation and on the Olympic franchises. We were charging double commissions, through me, I'm ashamed to say. But it wasn't just the double dipping. It was those damn microchips." Then he said almost to himself. "They know it in Israel. There are letters in the Israeli files."

Treason? Sara thought. "It probably was the KGB Ephraim. It was the KGB," she said, desperately, fervent in her desire to have it so.

"No, Sara. The CIA got there first. I'm convinced of it."

"But he worked with the CIA, Ephraim. You're saying they killed him for corruption? That's not reason enough."

"He worked for himself. He used their framework. He manipulated the CIA as he manipulated everyone else. Including me."

"You're saying he made you corrupt too?" she said accusingly. "That's...That's a disgusting excuse."

Ephraim nodded. "Saul was a sociopath. It's catching. The ability to rationalize to have no conscience, to feel only one's own suffering."

"You're saying you're the victim?" she said resentfully.

"We're all the victims."

Sara was shaking her head reflexively. She could not stop.

"Saul was like a pin point, the center. He was the ultimate fixer," Ephraim went on. "Geometric circles rippled from him. I was one of the ripples, and an evil one at that."

"Ripples, victims," she said, her anger returning in force. "My father was the ultimate victim, maybe of his own nature, but victim he was. Not me. Not you, Ephraim." She was glaring at him.

"Ah, Sara. Don't look at me like that. I truly loved him, in my way." He stood up. "I'll leave you now. You'll be all right?" he asked kindly, standing over her.

"Where will you go?"

"Back home to Israel. At least, I'm going to try."

"Are you a good enough Jew to be accepted there, after all the shady deals you pulled for my father?" she said bitterly.

"I'm a better Jew than yesterday," he said soberly, " because Saul Mammon is gone." Ephraim turned and walked from the conference room for the last time.

Chapter Twenty-Three

As Sara let herself into the apartment's elegantly rounded foyer she noticed a white envelope on the table. The handwriting on it was her mother's.

"You want drink?" Renata was standing unsteadily in the doorway to the salon. She was in one of her revealing caftans, this one in almost transparent shocking pink.

Sara shook her head.

"I need a drink," Renata said, saluting her with a brandy snifter filled almost to the brim.

"I see you do," said Sara coldly, picking up the envelope.

"That came earlier. Delivery boy. Is from your new lover, *hein*?" She started down the hall to her room.

"I ask you something?"

Sara turned, "What?"

"He was just lying across the chair?" Renata looked wobbly.

Sara stared at this odd apparition.

"Saul. That night…"Renata said, eyes bleary.

"Yes," her tone cutting.

"I'm a nervous wreck."

"I can see that."

"Where's the will? Renata demanded. "What about my settlement? You're his heir."

"There is no estate as such," Sara said evenly. "My father lived on expense accounts."

"You make this up. Hah! What about new yakt?" Renata said triumphantly. "He just buy it last year."

"The boat is owned by three different corporations."

Renata looked confused. "What about all the money from Russian Olympics?"

"What money?"

"Franchise money."

"Tell me something, Renata" said Sara. "How'd you pay your bills?"

"Like everyone else. With credit cards. We have dozens."

Sara could not help but laugh. "When the credit card bills came in, how were they paid?"

"One of Saul's secretaries. She'd go over and pay cash."

"And the food bills?"

Renata was growing more annoyed. "Saul give me money every month. Hundred dollar bills, or francs. I just go to various stores."

Sara was laughing full out.

"What's the matter with this?" Renata shouted. "We are never overdue."

"It's a great way of hiding your cost of living from the taxman."

"*Gott in Himmel,*" Renata yelled, her face livid.

"Just cool down, Renata."

"You make me sound like horse after race."

This threw Sara into another fit of laughter. She turned on her heel and moved down the hall.

"You laugh at me," shrieked Renata, and Sara heard the salon door slam shut as she entered the beige sanctuary of her bedroom, where abruptly she stopped laughing and flung herself clumsily on the bed, fully clothed, shoes and all, her purse half open on the floor. The envelope rested on her stomach as she lay in the dark, an arm across her eyes. After several minutes, she propped herself up on one elbow, turned on the bedside lamp, and slowly opened the envelope. In her mother's finest scrawl, she found the following:

Dec. 28

Sara darling,

Never for one second doubt your father loved you. You were the most important thing in his life. His future.

But he had a compulsion to punish those closest to him. He just did not understand, ever, what he did, the consequences of his actions. He made people feel disposable, and that's dangerous.

I'm planning to stay over a couple of days. Tomorrow, if you can, we could have the whole day together. Meet me at Hotel Bellegarde, rue des Beaux Arts, early. We can poke around, maybe have dinner later at a little place on rue Mazarine where Saul and I went on our honeymoon. It's still in business, as are all good things French.

Please come, darling. You've been slumming too long with your father's cronies, and with that handsome newspaperman. (Yes, I saw something between you at your father's service.)

Mostly, we'll talk. Love you,
Mama

December 29th, 1979

Chapter Twenty-Four

The next morning was cool and gray. Shortly after 10:00, Sara's taxi wove through the traffic, over the Pont Neuf, the cars like scurrying ants, and onto the Left Bank. Through a tight maze of streets off the Place St. Germain, the taxi found the rue des Beaux Arts, and Hotel Bellegrade. Off the entrance, opposite the concierge's office where a pretty red-haired receptionist sat, Anna was waiting.

"Mmm. Your checks are so cold. Have you eaten anything?" Sara shook her head.

Anna led her to the hotel restaurant at the rear of the building. It had been the original garden of the house, now enclosed, with the typically French 19th century white tin ceiling. They sat at a pink clothed table for two. A fountain against the back wall emitted a soothing plash. A young waiter approached.

"Nicholas, *café au lait, croissants, du beurre, la confiture, s'il vous plaît.*"

Nicholas nodded with a smile and disappeared.

"I'm so glad for this day," Sara said.

"I am too. I had to stay. I'm here for you, darling."

"I know," the girl said sadly, feeling vulnerable and about 12 years old. She felt a little unkempt in the same old suit. Her mother's chic always intimidated her.

"Come home with me."

"I can't. Besides, I see the police tomorrow."

"I'm sorry you have to go through that. I'll go with you, if you want." Sara shook her head.

"I think you're very brave," her mother remarked.

They finished their breakfast in silence. Hailing a taxi, they drove through the streets to *L'Hôtel Biron*, the house where Rodin had resided and worked, now his museum, on rue de Varenne. They walked through the tall swathed rose brushes over which the statue of Balzac, the ugly but powerful bronze in his robe to cover his nakedness, presided.

Inside the house, the stone floors had been worn smooth by Rodin's foot, his sculptures gathered in high-ceilinged rooms. Sara found some of the white marbles, extremely sexual. She thought of Denys. This angered her, and she could not look at her mother. She was grateful that Anna was deeply immersed in viewing some of the other artists' paintings on the walls that Rodin had collected, Gauguin in particular.

"Come now," Anna said slipping her arm through Sara's, after an hour or more. "Let's do a little shopping. Enough of this Left Bank." At Hermès, the elegant store on rue Faubourg St. Honoré, Anna bought a silk scarf in dark red and gold against a white ground. "No, don't wrap it, please," she said to the sales girl, as she it tied it in an ascot around Sara's throat, instantly transforming her black suit.

In a draped room, off the Ritz garden, as Anna, and her daughter lunched on *oeuf en gelée* and monkfish in a dill sauce, Anna proceeded to ask Sara about Denys Déols.

"I met him in Daddy's office," Sara mumbled, flushing. "He was doing some article or other about Saul Mammon."

"I saw one of those articles."

"He was not my father's friend," Sara said loudly.

"I think maybe he was just doing his job."

"But some of the things he wrote."

"I know, darling, but unfortunately, some of them are true."

"It's mostly innuendo, some of it scurrilous." Sara was growing agitated.

"Oh, I don't know about that. Le Monde is a very reputable publication. They wouldn't permit unscrupulous reporting."

"Well, it's all just strictly rumor. I'm sure of it."

"He's attractive," Anna remarked.

"Oh, I guess so – if you like a man who smells of tobacco."

"You've gotten that close?"

"You can't miss that smoky smell," Sara exclaimed. In fact, she had found that it only added to his appeal.

"You don't find him attractive?"

"Look. He infuriates me. He's just too…too…direct."

"I always thought being direct was, well, rather a sterling attribute," Anna said with a smile.

"Hey, it's not funny. Too direct is not 'sterling.'"

"I guess not. But well, I have to say, I thought you rather liked him. There seemed something intimate between you."

"Intimate?" Sara's stomach turned over.

"Yes. Just the way he touched your arm."

"Oh, please!"

"I think he likes you a lot. He couldn't take his eyes off you. Are you in love with him?" Anna asked softly.

"Good God." Sara burst out.

"Then why are you turning red?"

"Your questions embarrass me."

"Ah, I'm sorry. I don't mean to. It's just that I sensed the attraction. He's an interesting man."

"Who says?"

"I do," said Anna, as she paid the check. "And I should know," she added with a twinkle.

To change the subject, Sara began to speak with animation of her love of art. "I'm trying to see everything, all I can, from The Louvre to the smallest ateliers and Mama, I am trying to sketch Daddy's face."

"You're what?"

"I want to catch his face, his expression."

"That's impossible," said Anna under her breath,

"Why?"

"He was a chameleon."

"Well, I'm trying. I tried to give him his picture, the first one, as a little present. He didn't seem to care. But after… you know what happened?" She paused. "I found he did keep it."

After a moment, Anna said, "I want you to promise me something." She looked concerned.

"What, Mama?"

"I want you to go somewhere, anywhere. France is full of enchanting places, even at this time of year."

"I can't go away now," she said abruptly.

'You must. Just for a few days. After you speak with the police. I don't think you realize how traumatic this has been for you. And you're still living in the apartment with that awful woman."

"Yes," said Sara. "Yonka Doodle Dandy."

Anna laughed. "What? Is that what you call Renata?"

"No, Daddy did." Then Sara said, her voice somber, "I think I do understand the trauma. I really do"

"I don't believe you realize the depth," Anna said with a sigh. "Sometimes you're so grown up, mature and other times, it's like you're still a little girl. This event, it was shattering for you. I want you to get away…off by yourself. Just for a little while. Sit by the sea somewhere and paint and eat, you're thin, and just BE for a few days." She took Sara's hand, as tears formed in her daughter's dark eyes. "If you won't come home with me, will you at least do this?" Anna asked earnestly.

Sara nodded assent.

They walked down by the Seine in the late afternoon sun, which had peeped through for the moment. The old public buildings of Paris rose above the steely water of the river. The *Bateau Mouche* still plied around the Île St. Louis, glass enclosed in December, and the people on the bridges waved to the tourists, gliding on the river below.

Standing with their elbows on the parapet of the Pont Neuf as dusk descended over the city, a gentle cold crept in upon them. They had not spoken in some time, when Anna declared, "I must tell you a little story."

"About Daddy?"

Anna nodded in the twilight. "We were in New York, at a small Italian place, an after-dinner night spot called The Casanova, all dark velvet and red shaded little lamps. We had only been married four months. We were all drinking champagne, another couple, Saul and me. It was near midnight. A little man in a seedy tuxedo with a violin came to our table and said to your father, 'Your wish, Signore?' Saul said, 'A song?' The man nodded. I asked for 'Anima e Core,' 'Heart and Soul.' So Saul said to the man, 'You heard the lady, 'Anima e Core.' The little man beamed and put the violin under his chin, quite ecstatic because he was proud of the popular Italian song. Then Saul said to him, 'But I want you to play it off key.' 'Pardon, Signore?' said the old man astonished. 'You heard me. Play off key.' 'Saul,' I protested. 'Well, do you want this or not?' Saul said, waving a $100 bill at the musician. The little man turned white. He looked at the money and then slowly started, in the most humiliating way, to begin the melody, agonizingly off key. Everyone at our table laughed but me. It was so disrespectful, so cruel."

There was silence between mother and daughter on the bridge as the Seine gleamed below.

They returned to Hotel Bellegarde by taxi, which Sara planned to keep to take her home to the Right Bank. "*Attendez*," she told the driver as she stepped out of the car with her mother.

The hotel door was locked. Anna rang the night bell. The

red-haired receptionist in panty hose and rust colored sweater came running from the rear, flushed and disheveled. She opened the door with a smile, her lipstick smeared from ear to ear. Sara could see, through the long hall to the bar-restaurant, Nicholas, their waiter from breakfast. His tie was askew, shirt unbuttoned to the waist.

Anna turned to Sara with a little shrug as the girl disappeared toward Nicholas and the kitchen, her rounded bottom bouncing eagerly.

"Ah, well," she said. "Paris." Then, suddenly turning solemn, she embraced her daughter.

"Promise me you'll take some time away, darling," she whispered into Sara's hair.

"I will."

"And promise me one more thing," her mother said, leaning back and looking Sara in the face. "Never...ever...ask anyone to play off key."

December 30th, 1979

Chapter Twenty-Five

S ara was shattered after she returned from the police station to number 17, avenue Foch. Although she was under no personal suspicion, the police questioned her all morning in the greasy precinct of the 16th Arrondissement. She went through it all in a daze, repeating, it seemed interminably, what she had seen the night when she had entered her father's bedroom.

The police believed the theory that Saul Mammon's death was cardiac arrest. They had brushed over the blood on the chair, the crack in the larynx, the broken glasses. There was no sign of poison in the system. Ephraim had said there would not be. She never mentioned the gun that had been in his open suitcase, that she had handled it, that it was no longer there a few hours later when she returned to find him dead. That was her secret with Denys.

She thought she was alone in the big apartment. It was near two o'clock in the afternoon. Hearing voices from the servants' quarters, she went back to Claus' small cubicle beyond the pantry. The door was open. Peering into the room, Sara saw Renata and Claus entwined together under a sheet, their guttural grunts echoing into the kitchen.

"God!" Sara burst out.

They sat up red-faced and so startled, Claus leapt out of bed, throwing Renata off him. He was naked.

"Daddy's barely cold, " Sara shouted at them, outraged, slamming the door. She ran down the hall to her room, tripping over her own feet in her haste. Renata! The police were permitting her to remain in the apartment until the monthly lease was up February 1ˢᵗ, in spite of the fact she was not 'family.' Renata had crammed herself into her pimp's bed.

The phone on the bedside table was ringing as she ran into her bedroom. She picked it up. It was her mother.

"I'm catching the one o'clock plane to New York tomorrow, unless you need me to stay."

"No. No. It's okay." It was hard for Sara to speak. She was still sputtering inside over the vision of Claus naked and Renata,, frizzy hair askew.

"I loved our day together. You don't know what it meant to me." Anna hesitated, listening to Sara breathing. "Are you all right?"

Sara said nothing, shaking her head to dispel the ugly picture she had just witnessed.

"Are you there, Sara?" Her mother sounded alarmed.

"Do you want anything, I mean of his?" Sara asked, finally.

Anna was silent for a long time. "What do you mean?"

"I mean anything, well, personal? like….oh, I don't know," Sara stumbled on, "Like his opera tapes? You know how he loved opera, or maybe that plaque from the Italian Government, the one he received for THE FREEDOM TRAIN?"

Anna laughed softly "The Italian plaque?"

"Yes. You were married to him when it was given to him."

"Sara, I don't want to disillusion you any further, although Saul was deeply involved in THE FREEDOM TRAIN, when a plaque was given to Herman Tyson, chairman of the project, by the Italian Government, your father had one made up for himself."

Sara collapsed heavily on the edge of the bed.

"Well, I'm off … you know, last minute errands. I love you darling."

"And I love you, Sara mumbled."

She sat, arms wrapped around herself, now trying to shut out further thoughts of her father's deceptive self-aggrandizement. The plaque. Another fake? Renata's fake fur. Fake Vlaminck? Fake millions. Fake apartment. Fake yacht.

Her mind began to drift, growing vague. She wondered if Manny would be on the same plane as her mother. She wondered if Ephraim was on his way to Israel. She would probably never again see the Israeli who had laid on her such terrible knowledge. With his vast political sophistication and more important, his questionable morality, Sara had believed in him absolutely and his Bulgarian Method.

The phone rang again. It sounded like ice clattering. It rang several times before she picked up the receiver.

"Sara?" It was Denys Déols' anxious voice.

She slowly returned the receiver to its cradle. He was too mixed into her emotions. Somehow Denys Déols was involved in it all. His instincts about Saul Mammon had been right, but, at the moment, this fact revolted her.

She stood up. Her knees almost gave way. He mother was right. She had to flee to be alone somewhere, where perhaps she could sleep. She went to the closet, took out the suitcase and threw into it a few clothes from the bureau, jeans, a skirt, some shirts, a long cardigan the color of wine. She made a call to the Hertz office in the Coeur d'Or Hotel and arranged for a Volvo with a stick shift to be picked up in an hour. She didn't know where she was going. She was just going.

As she finished stuffing the small suitcase, was just snapping shut the clasps, Renata appeared in the doorway in a short terrycloth robe, which showed her knobby knees. She carried a half-full snifter of brandy in one hand and a cigarette in the other.

"Going back to New York?"

Sara did not respond. She busied herself distractedly with toilet articles on the dressing table, her hair brush, a bottle of cologne which she dropped to the floor and had to pick up.

Renata regarded her with curiosity. "Where then?" she asked.

Sara didn't answer as she jammed cold cream and powder and aspirin into a cosmetic kit.

"Where?" Renata repeated.

"Honfleur." It just burst out of her. Until that minute, she hadn't given a thought to where she would drive in the Volvo.

She turned to Renata. "And you, Fraulein? When do you return to Frankfurt? And do you take your arranger/lover with you?"

Insults never bothered Renata. She strolled across the room, a little drunk, and plunked down on the bed. "Don't worry. We never meet again. Claus and I, we go, but not to Frankfurt." She buried her lips in the brandy snifter.

"Without the pot of gold you were counting on."

"In East Berlin what good is pot of gold?"

"East Berlin?" Sara was stunned.

"*Yah.*"

She reopened the suitcase and was trying to stuff in the cosmetic kit. Her movements were full of fits and starts, attempting to digest this new bit of cross-Curtain information.

East Berlin. Renata conning the con man. Or was it vice-versa? Her father must have known? Or had he?

"I'm sorry you hate me so," said Renata.

"Well, what did you expect?"

The round blue eyes looked wistful. It only angered Sara the more. "I cared about your father." She sounded maudlin.

"He's barely dead and you're screwing the chauffeur," Sara said with disgust.

"I did love Saul."

"Well, you hardly showed it when he was alive, certainly not after his death," Sara retorted bitterly. "Always out dancing, drinking carrying on, 'hearing the beat.' The far side of the Berlin Wall doesn't have many discotheques, does it?" she continued through clenched teeth. "Wanting to know your settlement right in the middle of the

Memorial Service!" Sara was shouting at her. "Well the settlement's nothing." She turned to the woman on the bed and saw two enormous tears. "Do I see signs of sorrow, or is it guilt?"

"I wanted to be his wife."

"I don't doubt it. You thought he was rich."

"He lifted me up, made me feel like a queen. You don't understand what went on with Saul and me."

"How true." Sara was whacking the suitcase, trying to shut it again. "I sure don't."

"It was strange what we had."

"It was in bed, what you had."

"*Yah.* I give him something you could never," Renata said without a sign of smugness.

Sara slapped the suitcase so hard, it finally shut.

"I slowed him down," Renata went on. "I do him little dances. He liked that, you know, with garter belt. And he was good to me, kept me well, gave me things, maybe fake things, but still, the real things Saul was saving them for you. To Saul, you were most important – how you say – tie in life."

Renata's words shook Sara. "You come in here and weep and tell me this," she said. "Is it to flatter me? Why don't you go back to the servants' quarters where you belong."

She grabbed her suitcase, sketchbook, a handful of charcoal pencils, her wallet with its credit cards and Manny's hundred dollar bills. She slammed out of the bedroom door and down the hall, her feet clumping loudly through the foyer, into the elevator, through the courtyard and out onto the street where she hailed a taxi to take her to the Coeur d'Or garage.

Why had she decided to go to Honfleur? She had been there with her father some years ago, and it was DamnDéols birthplace. In late December, it would be cold and wet at the rocky seaport. It was as good a place as any.

By four o'clock, Sara had picked up the Volvo and a map. The stick shift felt good in her hand, a tangible connection to reality. She headed northwest, following the line of the Seine. She drove fast. She arrived at Rouen where she ate supper at a restaurant on the square, The Vieux Marché, where Joan of Arc was burned. She could barely taste the *steak/frites* and *Pinot Noir* wine.

She couldn't help but think of Denys, perhaps because she was headed for Honfleur. She had asked him to write about Manny Kiser for her own personal vengeance. She had tried to manipulate him to 'play off key.' But unlike Mama's violinist at The Casanova, Denys Déols had refused to compromise himself. She had behaved just like her father. That realization filled her with self-disgust.

It was dark when she came out of the small restaurant. Continuing north through Normandy, she turned before Le Havre toward Honfleur, at the mouth of the Seine where it ran into the sea. The port was not far from the invasion of World War II, Omaha Beach, Utah Beach, such American names. In the darkness, the historic countryside through which she drove so swiftly seemed haunted by spirits.

She found a room on the second floor of an inn on the waterfront. There was freshness in the air from the open window. She slept that night the sleep of the exhausted, for the first time in weeks, without dreams.

The New Year

Chapter Twenty-Six

The inn was an old, narrow house, *L'Auberge de Côte de Grâce*, named for the protective circle of hills. The old port was famous for its broiled fish and *moules marinières*, also for its *Calvados*, the apple brandy of the region, which warmed fingers and toes.

As one day passed, two days, three, she was aware her head was starting to clear, and she felt less old. No one approached her, the French being civilized enough to leave one alone.

She sketched the sea every day, and on this fourth morning, she sat in the gray light on the end of the pier in her wine colored cardigan. She was trying to capture on paper the mood of the sea. The cormorants with eyes like marbles wheeled above her head. They plunged for fish into the pewter waves whose shadows suddenly seemed to take on the configuration of her father's face. The charcoal in her hand, of itself, shifted the lines on the paper to the face of the man with the dimple in his cheek. She could not bear the things he had done, but she would always love him. She remembered the small apologetic smile that would cross his face when he suddenly realized how damaging were his own words.

Suddenly, Denys appeared, bringing a clutch to her heart as he bent down to her and sat beside her. They were like two children, his long legs next to hers, dangling over the edge of the pier toward the water. In silence, they watched the dark hulls of the fishing trawlers like a troop of slow-moving camels crossing a limitless gray desert.

"How did you find me?" she asked finally.

"I beat it out of Claus." Sara looked at him. "Nooo…not literally. I think he was glad to have me tracking you down, knew it would annoy you."

"It doesn't annoy me." But it did.

"I know you want to be alone."

"I'm not alone. You're here."

He leaned toward her face and started to kiss her. Their lips just touched before she pulled away.

"I can't."

"Nobody's looking," he said with a grin.

She didn't laugh, just looked straight ahead, "Somehow you're part of it."

"And proud to be," he said.

"Well, I'm not."

"Ah, Sara."

"No. You're part of it all."

"Of what?" He drew back, brows furrowed.

"You know. His…"

"Death?"

She nodded.

"How can I be part of it?" he said, slapping his brow. Denys always gesticulated a great deal.

"You're part of the events that brought it about. Your article made my father's position untenable."

"I didn't make his position untenable, Sara. He did that all by himself. It was bound to come out, the double-dealing. His death was going to happen sooner or later in similar circumstances. Everyone was breathing down his neck, not just me."

"I don't care about everyone else. I wasn't sleeping with everyone else. I was with you, and it was you who forced things into the open."

"I only told what I saw to be the facts. Look. I'm a professional. That's what I am and always hope to be. If you find this arrogant and unkind to your feelings, I'm sorry. But so be it. I try to tell the truth."

He sat beside her very still for a moment, then leapt to his feet and started walking back on the rocks that rose at the base of the pier, where the water foamed like white lace. She watched him treading carefully on the rugged shapes, his hands in the pockets of his corduroys, head down, hair blowing. As he progressed farther down near the water line, as the hunched figure grew smaller in the distance, she could bear no longer the sight of him disappearing.

"Wait," she cried, jumping up and running after him. "Wait for me."

———

She sat in the armchair in her room on the second floor of the inn, curled up before a fire in the small grate. Denys was on the small settee adjacent to the hearth. The flames provided the only light in the room whose corners disappeared into the shadows. They each held a glass of *Calvados*. She had donned his old, worn sweater. She had not yet given him the new sweater-replacement, because Christmas had come and gone in horror.

"He was not one man, but a composite," Denys said to the ceiling. "The genius, the fraud, the adventurer, the crook, the generous cheat." With each attribute he ticked off, eyes squinting, another puff from his *Gauloise* moved upward.

"Whatever the situation called for, he would fill it," Sara said, rousing up. "Did you know he was a member of the American Communist Party as a young man? Then he turned into a fascist in middle age, and was living like a Russian prince when he died. He confused himself with some great force of nature, but we, he and I, we never had a real confrontation. He died too soon." She rose and went to the bottle of *Calvados* on the small table near the door, disappearing into the edges of darkness, returning with the bottle in hand.

"And now, *ma belle*, what is it we do about it," he said in his accented English.

"Do?" She stood there..

"You are convinced it was murder. So am I. There are others who think so too, of that I'm sure."

Sara paused. "I know of at least one."

"Renata, eh?"

She shook her head and poured apple brandy into his glass, more into her own. She sat cross-legged on the small rug at his feet, the bottle on the floor beside her.

"Ephraim Bachman."

"The Israeli?"

She stretched back on her palms and in a low voice, told Denys exactly what Ephraim had spoken of that day in the conference room of her father's office. Denys leaned forward, eyes fixed on her moving lips.

"It must have been exactly as Ephraim said. The Bulgarian Method."

"I've heard of it,' Denys exclaimed soberly.

"Perpetrated by The Company."

"The CIA? He said that? I always thought it possible."

"That's what Ephraim thinks. I can see it. A man sitting in a Peugeot parked opposite number 17. I can see him slip between the buildings into the narrow alley, you know, where Claus parks the limousine. I can see him climb the back fire escape like a cat, reaching the third floor, making his way around the building on the cornices."

"Oh, Sara, don't do this," Denys said, alarmed by her demeanor.

She was up and pacing, agitated, quite beside herself. "I can picture his face, the glittering eyes. He would reach my father's balcony. The French door was always ajar. My father liked a cool room at night, and his music, Wagner's 'Götterdammerung,' that's what he was playing on the stereo."

"Sara, you must stop."

"My father would come from the bathroom after his shower, just as the man pushed in the French door. Can you imagine the shock? 'Who the hell are you?' Or maybe he even recognized the man."

Denys was on his feet beside her. "Stop this now. Just stop."

"Daddy would edge around him, almost reaching the revolver in his suitcase. I told you it was there, didn't I?"

Denys' hands were on her shoulders. "You cannot do this." But nothing could arrest her momentum.

"The man would give Daddy a karate chop to the throat, the poisonous soaked handkerchief over the nose – heart stopped."

Denys was speechless, caught up in this obsessive recitation of the death of Saul Mammon.

"The Bulgarian Method. That's what it was. The killer would go to the suitcase and pocket the gun, go to the stereo and switch it to high, full blast. That's what made me come running, but of course, the man was long gone into the wet night, and my poor father dead upon the chair, cut down ..."

They sank to the hearthrug, he rocking her. She was almost incoherent. He murmured words in French meant to soothe and later she fell asleep.

With dawn, a steel-like color crept between the blinds. Denys and Sara rose stiffly from the floor where they had lain through the night, and fell into deep slumber on top of the bed, with arms around one another. How she clung to him.

Sara awoke before he did. She went to the round table beneath the window and sat on a straight chair, elbows on the tabletop. In a certain way, the dramatic incantation had brought catharsis. She was numb, and she knew her father was gone.

When Denys awoke, she fixed *café au lait* on the hot plate with milk purchased yesterday. There were dark circles beneath her eyes. Besides the large coffee cups on the table lay her sketchpad. It was open and there, face up, was the portrait of Saul Mammon.

"May I close this?" he asked all politeness.

She nodded.

But first he looked at the drawing. "You know this is remarkable." He laughed. "He certainly looks important, like a very rich man."

"He sure acted like one, but all was illusion. Manny Kiser told me he's going to file for bankruptcy."

"You mean you're a poor girl? Wonderful." He grinned as he closed the top of the sketchpad, shutting off her father's face, "I like poor girls. Who did Saul Mammon think he was, I wonder?"

"Saul Mammon!" said Sara, suddenly giddy. "Nobody else." She reached for her wallet. It was in the string bag on a chair next to the table. She opened it and extracted her credit cards. She fanned them out, waved them in the air and threw them toward the ceiling. They fell in plastic lumps about the room. "I won't be needing these," she said. "I'm sure I can't afford 'em." The gesture was so unexpected, they both fell to laughing. Sara, still practical, did not do the same with Manny's hundred dollar bills still in their bank wrappers in her bag.

"Oh, I love to have you laugh." Denys said happiness spreading over his face.

"I'm okay," she said.

"It may be too soon, but I'd like to ask you a question," he said solemnly.

She nodded.

"Are you prepared to go forward?"

She looked at him, perplexed.

"To pursue the truth with me?"

She looked at him seriously. "No. Denys I don't think so."

"But…Sara …" Her face showed such conviction he said no more. She got up from the table and put on her wine colored cardigan again. They walked on the street before the inn, that gray, cold day, past old houses facing the wharf, where nets were hung to dry on tall rafter-like scaffolds. They went past fish merchants selling cod, and herring, and sardines from the icy ocean. He showed her the stone house on avenue La Busse where he was born. Then he took her by a narrow dark lane to a small shop where he bought her a gathered peasant skirt. It was long, of black cotton, and strewn with tiny pink flowers.

There was a steamboat just leaving for Le Havre across the water, and another distant steamer coming from that town. They watched the two ships pass each other going in opposite directions. The steamboats disappeared into two separate horizons. She looked sorrowfully at Denys. "I'll be going home soon."

"You are giving up," he said sadly.

"I have to. It's just too painful."

They were walking slowly from the high ground back to the center of town. The wind blew colder.

"You were so ready to do battle. What about the Bulgarian Method?"

"I have no heart for it anymore."

"Then you return to the States without knowing the truth."

"I do know the truth and there's nothing I can do about it."

"What about the killer?"

"To hell with him."

"I thought you were more your father's daughter," he said with irritation.

"DamnDéols. That's emotional blackmail."

"*Peut-être*. But it's also true. I thought you had more of the Mammon juggernaut in you. Where is that Mammon woman now?"

Sara walked quickly toward the inn. He rushed his steps to keep up with her,

"Just how are you going to forget?" he called into the wind.

"I'll just forget," She yelled back.

As she collected her things in the second floor bedroom, he pressed further.

"You can't just turn tail and run away, back to the States."

"I have a job."

'That's an excuse, Sara. You told me you had leave for three months. It's been less than one since you arrived in Paris." He took her by the shoulders, turning her to him.

"The truth, Sara. What else is there?"

"Maybe it's best not to know it."

He shook his head solemnly. "I for one cannot let that go. If the truth comes back to hurt and haunt you, I'm sorry, but I must bring these things out."

"Don't, please."

"I must."

He moved away from her and sat in the armchair before the fireplace where they had communed so deeply the previous night. She went over to him there, getting on her knees at his feet. "Let me forget. Don't write any more articles. Promise me you won't."

"I can't promise that."

"I thought you cared about me, even a little."

"I do. Perhaps more than you know."

"Than do this for me. Let it be. Be my friend. Let's make love," she said suddenly. "Do you want to make love?" She pulled at his hand, her smile overly bright.

He shook his head." Ah, Sara. Not this way. Not as some sort of bribe. That's not making love."

His words shook her. She was suddenly cold all over, disgusted with herself. "You'd best leave."

He got up and went to the doorway, leaving her crouched on the hearthrug. His eyes were shiny,

"I'll go," he said quietly. "But I cannot do as you ask. I'm going to Paris and straight-away, I will pick up the telephone, call the American Embassy and make an appointment with the Executive Officer of the G2 Staff. His name is Cutter. Ephraim Bachman believed it was The Company. Saul Mammon's contact was Cutter."

"No. Don't."

"I must."

"No."

"Yes." Denys Déols turned and closed the door behind him.

January 1st, 1980

Chapter Twenty-Seven

Sara's Volvo entered Paris early in the morning. She had driven slowly from Honfleur, her judgment clouded with feelings for Denys Déols, the man from Honfleur, his persona, the flashes of gentleness, the sexuality that had triumphed between them. She wore the flowered skirt he had given her. His stubbornness and determination had brought her to her knees. She had lost him to his crusade, this man, the pivotal other in her world. Her two men were gone. She drove through Neuilly-Sur-Seine and into Paris by way of the Porte de Ternes. The river was like glass.

Turning onto the Champs-Elysées, Sara headed for the Coeur d'Or Hotel. She left the Volvo in the garage, there, then picked up a copy of Le Monde, and found a taxi. "*Dix-sept*, avenue Foch," she told the driver.

How she dreaded facing Renata and Claus. In the taxi, she regarded Le Monde with suspicion. Curiosity made her turn to the Op-Ed page. "THE MYSTERIOUS DEATH OF SAUL MAMMON." That was the title Denys Déols had given this latest feature. She glanced at the article. Apparently, he had tried to see Cutter, who he referred to as a "player in the American Intelligence hierarchy," but, in the article, he claimed he was rebuffed summarily and was unable to interview the man. Toward the end of the article, she noticed the line: "Saul Mammon left a murky legacy to the world." DamnDéols. Yet, she was in for a stronger shock, his final paragraph.

> "The American Embassy claims Saul Mammon died simply of cardiac arrest. Why then have the police sent his body to the Institut Medico-Legal which only receives bodies classified HOMICIDES BY PERSONS UNKNOWN?"

Sara threw the newspaper on the seat beside her. So Déols was not able to get to Cutter! He could not confront the G2 agent with his suspicions. Her eyes stared through the dirty cab window at the Paris streets. She saw nothing but the word homicide etched into the dust on the window, and suddenly, Sara knew exactly what she had to do.

When the taxi arrived at number 17, there was a large, white van parked in front of the courtyard entrance. On its side were the words, *Meuble en Transit* in black letters.

Sara went up to the apartment, dreading every step. The massive front door with its brutal locks was wide open. Three men from the moving company in work clothes and dark blue aprons were crating the wild animal figurines in the long hall. She stood there, watching Claus giving orders in broken French. Renata stood next to him in jeans and shirt. She almost looked normal.

"*Ach,*" she said, on seeing her standing there.

"What's going on?"

"What's look like? They go to auction…to pay your father's debts."

Another moving man came out of the salon carrying the Vlaminck. He left it in the hall to be encased and returned to the green and gold room, only to return with the Ormolu mantle clock. Sara looked into the salon to see a woman, wrapping the glasses and crystal decanters from the bar in tissue paper and placing them in a carton at her feet.

"I won't be long," she said to Renata, brushing past her and moving down the hall to her bedroom. The clothes she had so carefully chosen and brought to Europe were in the closet. She decided to leave them there. She wanted them no more. She stood in the middle of the room and looked at it one last time, then went into the red-carpeted hall, irresistibly drawn to her father's bedroom. The police wire was again across the door closure. This time, with a nail scissor, she clipped the wire and walked boldly into the brown room. The impact of entering his death chamber took her breath away.

She wanted something of his. Anything. And then she saw his tape recorder resting beneath his desk between the French doors. She went to it, hesitant, flicked it on. The machine whirred. The tape inside was blank. She picked it up and slipped it into the string bag. The small, portable carrying case for tapes was under the desk as well. She opened it. There she found several cassettes, packed in neat rows, labeled with his favorite operas, mostly Wagner, 'Lohengrin,' 'Tristan und Isolde,' 'Das Rheingold.' The space for 'Götterdammerung' was empty. That tape was still in the stereo. She shut the top of the case and picked it up by the leather handle. She noticed the last tie he wore, the striped one, lying on the desk. It looked so vulnerable. Next to it was the tie tack. She hastily stuck the tiny device into her pocket.

"What you do? Renata stood by the door,

"What's it look like?"

"Stealing."

"You don't think these old opera recordings would bring anything at auction, now do you really?" Sara said gesturing with the case of cassettes, which was surprisingly heavy.

"Every time you come here, you cut police wire. They think it's me," Renata said peevishly. Good, Sara thought, let the police think Renata the thief.

Sara went past her and down the hall through the open front door, turning once to look back down the corridor. It was rapidly being dismantled. Her final view of the apartment at number 17, avenue

Foch was of a fat moving man removing THE FREEDOM TRAIN plaque from the Government of Italy from the wall.

Lugging her string bag, sketchpad, and tape case, Sara found a taxi, telling the driver to take her to The American Embassy. She was determined! Resolved! If the journalist, Denys Déols, was unable to see Cutter, she was sure she could. After all, she was Saul Mammon's daughter! She knew exactly what she was going to say, and, more important, she was going to get DamnDéols the scoop of his life!

———

Elliott Cutter. One of the Bobbsey twins. Sara recognized him from the Memorial Service. He was the one who wore the yellow socks. He sat at his plain desk before a window through which a muted sunlight drifted. Behind him was the American flag, the pole capped with the replica of an eagle. There had been no problem seeing him. She was Sara Mammon, a sensitive player.

Cutter cleared his throat. "The official autopsy report from the Institut Medico-Legal is right here in front of me." His signet ring caught glints of sunlight as he riffled the papers. "You know the body's been delivered there. It was a heart attack. Here," he said, peering at the top sheet in front of him. "It says, 'Cardiac lesions sufficient to cause death.'"

"What about the blood on the chair?"

"That could have been…er…a pre-attack nose bleed…or the blow when he fell on the chair."

"What about the crack in his larynx?"

"Same thing again. Could've hit his neck on the back of the chair…you know…crushed in the fall…"

"That would have been some kind of contortion, wouldn't it?"

Her questions had all been rapid. Cutter's face held firm except he pursed his lips.

"And the broken glasses?"

"What is this, an interrogation?" The faceless Mr. Cutter in his gray suit seemed tense. Her father would have called him a nebbish.

"Yes. It's an interrogation. I'm his daughter. I have a right to know the truth."

He nodded briefly, shrugging, giving up.

"And the gun?" she said.

"There was no gun."

"I saw it in his suitcase earlier when I said goodnight to him."

"Now, Sara," Cutter said placatingly. "I may call you that mayn't I? After all, your father and I were friends."

"Friends?" she said quietly. "I thought you ran Saul Mammon." Cutter sat frozen in his chair.

"We were friends and associates. That's all. Whatever gave you such a dramatic idea? Ran him to do what?"

She didn't answer. She sat there and watched him.

"As for the gun," he went on nervously, "you mustn't let your imagination get inflamed. What you thought you saw...."

"It was the handle of a revolver under a shirt in his suitcase and I don't think I saw it. I saw it."

"It could've been the heel of a shoe."

"It wasn't. I picked it up."

Cutter got up from his chair. He went to the window, turned around and faced her. His stance seemed to give him extra strength. He was again wearing yellow socks. "The American Embassy here in Paris has sent confidential telexes – I'm only telling you this because you are Saul Mammon's daughter – to the Secretary of State in Washington, that it was a heart attack. The matter is closed."

"If it was just a heart attack, why isn't my father deep in the ground, not still lying on some stone plank at the Institut Medico-Legal. Answer me that, Mr. Cutter. Is it because the investigation is still pending?" She stood up. " It was murder."

"You can't go around saying that," he said angrily. "You can't begin such a rumor. It's a lie and a dangerous one. Saul Mammon's personal physician, Robillon, you know him, he had to sedate you," Cutter said pointedly. "Robillon *and* the French police surgeon who were both there immediately after it was reported, both declared it a heart attack."

"Mr. Cutter," Sara said very slowly. "Have you ever heard of The Bulgarian Method?"

There was dead silence. His face betrayed nothing.

"Do you read Le Monde, Mr. Cutter?"

He shook his head.

"Had you read today's, you might have noticed an article by Denys Déols which quotes a French law. In order for a body to be delivered to the Institut Medico-Legal, the case must be classified by French law, mind you, as Homicide by Persons Unknown. Homicide, Mr. Cutter, Homicide."

She turned, leaving him ashen and visibly shaken. She went out into the hall in front of his office. She thought her exit dignified, but now she found her palms sweaty, and she leaned back against Cutter's closed door, clutching her string bag, sketchbook and the tape case.

Chapter Twenty-Eight

Denys Déols was not at home. Sara found herself once more perched on the curb, string bag and sketch book in hand, the cassette case on the pavement, before the imposing black door. It was dark and cold. "DamnDéols. I'm not through with you."

She did not see him approaching from La Place de La Bastille until he was almost upon her. She was only a small shape huddled on the ground but when she rose, her hands on her hips, he started to run the last steps.

He took her in his arms. They hung on to one another, a warmth suffusing arms and legs and faces, one against the other. They went directly upstairs to his apartment and into his bedroom. He picked her up and laid her on this counterpane. He undressed her slowly, the blouse, the flowered skirt, then lay beside her, and gently began to make love.

"You're here. You're here with me. You're staying," he murmured, stroking her face.

"For a while," she said.

Near midnight, from the kitchen, Denys brought some cheese, a *baguette* and a smoky glass carafe of wine, which they passed between them.

Sara sat in the middle of the counterpane in his old sweater. The terms between them had shifted rapidly.

"You know what they say about the truth," she said, munching on small pieces of *gruyère* she broke off from the larger wedge. "It's supposed to set you free."

"As long as it doesn't set you free from me too soon," he said solemnly. His naked back rested against the ancient headboard. The counterpane reached up to his chest.

"It just might, you know. The truth. I don't know. Once things are clearer you might just get swept away with the rest of the debris."

"That's a marvelous thing to say. I hope it's not soon."

"DamnDéols. Truth is hard."

"It's worth it," he said emphatically. "You and I are different. You are Mammon's daughter. I, a journalist from another country, another culture, but now..." he said with a smile, " until I get – how did you say – 'swept away with the rest of the debris...'" and he reached for her again.

Toward dawn, Sara went into the living room, and returned with the tape recorder she had picked up in her father's bedroom and put in her string bag. She set it on the chair next to Denys. He was still deep in sleep. She sat on the bed next to him and watched him, smiling at the way his lashes would occasionally flutter. He must have felt her there for he reached a hand up to touch her face.

"Are you awake?" she whispered.

"I am now," he said rousing up.

"I have a present for you."

"What?" he grinned, looking pleased, running his hand through his hair.

"You're sure you're awake? You have to be for this."

"*Absolument.*"

She got up and pressed the 'Play' button on the tape recorder.

There was the sound of a male voice. Denys looked perplexed.

"It was a heart attack. Here..." the male voice said on the tape recorder. Sara had had the presence of mind to turn on the machine in her string bag set on her knees as she sat in front of Cutter's desk in his office at the American Embassy yesterday. The conversation was there, recorded with all its nuances.

"He never even knew it," she said proudly to Denys.

Denys Déols was listening intently, eyes alight. "*Dieu*," he said when he heard her question to Cutter: ' Have you ever heard of The Bulgarian Method?' He clapped his hands. "You dared to ask that, Sara? Sara! You are something!"

"I didn't wait to hear Mr. Cutter splutter when I said 'Homicide by Persons Unknown,' but as I walked out I could feel the daggers in my back. By the way, that phrase, 'Homicide by Persons Unknown,' in your last article…?"

"It's the law," he said, dead serious. He arose from the bed, wrapping the counterpane around his waist and went into the living room. She trailed after him. The cassette case was on the floor beside the lumpy sofa. Denys approached it gingerly as if it was going to explode.

"It's only opera tapes in there. Otherwise the police would have taken it," Sara said. "My father loved to play dramatic music at night." But Denys was looking intensely at the black cassette case.

"See?" she said. "This is where 'Götterdammerung' would be, here in this slot. I left it at the apartment. It was still in the stereo." His expression was so like a hunting dog pointing at the prey, she paused. "You don't think…?"

I wonder," he said pulling out 'Lohengrin' and slipping it into the recorder, pressing the 'Play' button.

It was not 'Lohengrin,' It was not Wagner. It was not music at all. It was her father's voice that filled the room, and it was mesmerizing.

But, of course! Daddy was obsessed with taping, she thought, especially with taping himself.

They listened rapt to the first tape, long conversations between Saul Mammon and Novikov, half in Russian, with an accented interpreter. Saul Mammon had obviously compromised the Soviet official to such a degree with bribery, that Novikov provided Saul with statistics on

Soviet mineral production, on the build-up of arms, even on wheat inventories. Why Novikov was as greedy as any capitalist tycoon!

There were conversations with other Russian men with unpronounceable names, in halting English, as Mammon threw out bits of information, figures on the US economy and policy changes in the White House, as teasers. These dialogues, some in Russian restaurants with tinny music in the background, were often frivolous, the officials seeking women of the evening. She heard her father expound on the ornamentation of the expensive Moscow apartment off Gorki Square where he promised welcome to these gentlemen as a trysting place. This Sara found disgusting.

Then followed a recording that must have been made with his tie tack bug. The words came through scratchy. It was Manny Kiser's voice.

I THINK WE'VE GOT HER SAUL. THERE'S NO WAY RENATA CAN GET AWAY WITH BLACKMAILING YOU. TROUBLE IS, YOU'VE TOLD HER TOO MUCH. ANYWAY, WE'LL SCARE HER TO DEATH, EVEN TAKE HER TO COURT ON DRUG CHARGES. WE'LL WAIT FOR A JUDGE WE CAN FIX. BUT DON'T WEAR AN EIGHTEEN HUNDRED DOLLAR SUIT AND YOUR PATEK PHILLIPE WATCH TO COURT. Manny paused. WE CAN ALWAYS SHIP HER BACK TO EAST BERLIN.

Saul Mammon's reply was a curt NO.

Her father was afraid of Renata. She must have had something on him, something that ran all the way behind the Iron Curtain. The former call girl from Frankfurt had had a hook in Saul Mammon's flesh,

Déols selected another tape, this time, 'Das Reingold.' Instead, it was a telephone call. First, there was a dial tone; then, the little beeps of digits being punched: finally Saul Mammon's voice on the whirring tapes.

HEY CUTTER. YA SCRAMBLED?

ALWAYS.

NOVIKOV'S COMING TO PARIS FOR A LEG OPERATION – PHLEBITIS – HE'LL BE HERE FOR A FEW MONTHS. IT MIGHT BE JUST THE TICKET TO HAVE HIM STAY ABOARD MY YACHT WHILE HE RECURPERATES THIS SPRING.

NO WAY.

HE'S MY MOLE, FOR CHRISSAKES.

IT'S IRONIC, SAUL, YOU THINK YOU'RE GOING TO CORRUPT HIM WHEN HE'S JUST WAITING FOR YOU TO RENOUNCE THE WEST.

YOU DON'T TRUST ME, DO YOU, CUTTER?

NEVER HAVE! YOU'RE TO CLOSE TO THE MOLE HOLE. NOVIKOV, EH? A HUMAN MICROCHIP, RIGHT, SAUL? OH YES, WE KNOW ALL ABOUT THE FALSE FLAG CRAP IN GENEVA WITH THE ISRAELI. WE'VE FORGIVEN YOU A LOT OF NONSENSE, SAUL. YOU'VE HAD A FREE PASS BECAUSE OF YOUR WASHINGTON CONNECTIONS. BUT NOT THIS NOVIKOV BUSINESS. GETTING CHUMMY WITH HIM ON YOUR YACHT? IT COULD DAMAGE THE U.S. GOVERNMENT.

HOW?

SAUL, WE KNOW HE DANCES TO YOUR PERSONAL TUNE.

THAT MAKES IT SUCH A GOOD IDEA.

THAT MAKES IT A LETHAL COMBINATION. HE'S A POWER IN THE KREMLIN, AND YOU'RE HIS GREAT BIG PAL. WE KNOW YOU AND HE SHIPPED SOVIET ARMS TO LIBYA. YOU GOT BEAUCOUP DOUGH FOR IT, DIDN'T YOU? YOU'RE GETTING SO BLATANT. YOU'D BETTER START WORRYNG.

ME WORRY? WHAT YA THINK YOU'RE GONNA DO, CUTTER?

DON'T TEMPT ME, SAUL. JESUS, THE TWO OF YOU ARE CAPABLE OF STARTING WORLD WAR THREE. JUST DO WHAT WE PAY YOU TO DO.

Saul Mammon's answer was soft. OR?
The receiver clicked off.

Chapter Twenty-Nine

Denys Déols' latest article on Saul Mammon appeared in <u>Le Monde</u> on January 8th, 1980. Sara sat on the lumpy couch in Denys' little salon. She picked up the newspaper from the coffee table. Denys watched her thoughtfully,

"THE SAUL MAMMON MYSTERIES," she said aloud, looking at the headlines. She put the paper down with a sigh.

Denys knew her well enough by now to realize she would not be able to resist, so he sat silently in the old easy chair, puffing his *Gauloise.*

"Mysteries, mysteries," she said, picking up the paper again.

"Every article I've written about him contained that word mysteries because he was surrounded by them in life and death."

"There's only one mystery. Who killed him?" she said bitterly.

'What about the why? Besides, there are brutal ambiguities about his death that required the word mysteries."

"For instance?"

"Mystery number one. Do you really think anyone could occupy such a position of confidence with the men in Moscow without being vetted thoroughly by the KGB?"

"I suppose not."

"Did they like him?"

"Who knows?"

"Did they trust him?"

Sara shook her head vigorously. "Hardly. Particularly after you blew their scoop on The Red Moon."

"He blew it, Sara. You know that. But there were far deeper reasons for distrust. Moscow gave him everything he wanted, a dazzling apartment in an old palace off Gorki Square with air conditioning and lavish chandeliers. He was most valuable to them, traveling to and from Moscow through the Curtain."

"Perhaps 'to' Moscow, but why 'from'?" she asked.

"Maybe he distributed disinformation to the West. And if you think that possible," Denys said, leaning forward and pointing to a paragraph in his article, "Mystery number two: Could anyone occupy such a position of confidence with the men in Washington without being vetted by the CIA? Did they like him?"

"I guess so."

"Did they trust him?

"They would have had to, in the beginning."

"Did the CIA consider him valuable 'from Moscow' but not 'to'?"

"Now I'm confused."

Denys sat back, smiling at her, then said seriously, "Sara, suddenly the man is dead in his own bedroom. That death warrants justice. The American Embassy claims he died simply of cardiac arrest, but you know they don't send a body to the Institut Medico-Legal unless there is a real question as to cause of death. There, they even do an autopsy."

Sara winced.

"You've suspected foul play," he went on. " I've suspected it as well, and obviously, the French authorities do too. Just look at Cutter's reaction and Bachman's response. You tell me whether there are mysteries or not."

Denys Déols' article on Saul Mammon was picked up by newspapers in Paris, starting that low hum of innuendo that Mr. Cutter, at the American Embassy had so longed to avoid. Moscow was silent. Saul Mammon's death had gone unreported in the U.S.S.R. In

Paris, television carried it on the evening broadcasts. Features were written about the "MYSTERIES." The people of Paris were convinced of shady dealings. Saul Mammon was murdered by the KGB. Saul Mammon was knocked off by the CIA. Saul Mammon was killed by disgruntled business associates, by Idi Amin, by Israeli Intelligence, by Yasir Arafat. Denys Déols was convinced the G2 men at the Embassy were desperately trying to hush the "MYSTERIES" in the States because they were involved in his death.

And Sara? She was terrified of what more the black cassette case might contain. It rested on the floor near the sofa.

On a cold January morning, she shook herself from bed, threw on his old sweater, lighted the gas heater in the kitchen, and put water on the stove for coffee. She had determined to hear the rest of her father's tapes. It seemed such an unfinished business.

She went into the living room. Denys already sat on the couch. It was as if he was waiting for the moment, although he had already listened to them when she was out. His news instinct had compelled it.

As she came through the doorway, he got up, selected a tape, 'Tristan and Isolde.' Of course, there was no music.

It was still a shock to her, to listen to her father's electronic voice. He was talking to himself, the permanent obsession, his words private, over the sound of water lapping in the background.

THIS YACHT, IT'S MY PREFERRED FORM OF DALLIANCE. PEOPLE FROM ALL OVER THE WORLD COME TO IT. DEALS ARE MADE OVER THE HAUT BRION AND LANGOUSTE, DEALS THAT HOLD, DEALS THAT ARE TANGLED, DELICATE. FOR ME, THE DEAL IS ALL.ON THIS BOAT...THEY ALL BUY INTO WHATEVER I'M SELLING.

Déols looked at her. "He certainly knew how to seduce."
The sun was coming over the chimney pots, through the church spires, slanting across la Place de La Bastille and settling into Denys

little living room, as Saul Mammon went on in communion with himself. Sara walked into the kitchen. She had forgotten the coffee. The water had boiled away. She heard her father's voice finish.

"There are only two left," Denys called.

"Play them," she said. "Let's get this over with." More water was simmering and she spooned some of the chicory-flavored grounds into the *filtre* compartment.

Suddenly Maria Callas' voice filled the apartment, a magnificent aria from 'Turandot.'

Sara poked her head into the salon with a grin. "Well what do you know? Music."

Denys shrugged. She returned to the stove as Callas' high note was cut off and was replaced by the final tape.

DO YOU KNOW, THIS PORTRAIT OF ME IS DAMN GOOD.

Her father's voice was soft from the next room. It was as if he was there, beckoning her. She dropped the bag of coffee. The grounds were strewn from one end of the kitchen to the other, her father's voice whispering to her through long shadows.

YOU JUST LEFT YOUR OLD MAN'S BEDROOM, KID, AND I MISS YOU ALREADY.

Sara stood frozen in the kitchen doorway,

THE MORE I LOOK AT THIS, THE BETTER ARTIST I KNOW YOU ARE. BUT USE PRETTY COLORS, SARA. THAT'S ALL THERE IS.

She visualized him, leaning back against the pillows on his bed.

YOU KNOW, IT DEPENDS WHAT YOU WANT KID. CAVIAR, SIRLOIN, AN ELEPHANT. WHEN YOU FIGURE IT OUT, YOU BITE. He chuckled. AN ELEPHANT. THAT'S WHAT I WANTED. THE BIGGER IT WAS, THE MORE TO GET YOUR TEETH INTO. YOU CAN TWIRL THE WORLD. YOU CAN CHIP AWAY AT IT. YOU CAN EXPEDITE, MANIPULATE, WORK THE STREETS AND AIRWAYS LIKE I DO. BUT REMEMBER, LITTLE GIRL, DON'T BE TOO MUCH LIKE ME. YOU'RE NOT JUST SAUL MAMMON'S KID. YOU'RE AN ARTIST. YOU ARE SARA MAMMON – AND THAT'S ENOUGH FOR ANYONE.

She could almost see him wink. But then his mood changed, his voice gruff.

IT'LL BE OVER ANY DAY NOW FOR ME. I KNOW IT.

She thought the tape was dead as she stood immobilized in the center of Denys' living room, but then she heard his last words, very soft,

IN THE MEANTINE, MERRY CHRISTMAS, KID.

Early Winter 1980

Chapter Thirty

Sara was still there in Denys' messy apartment. It was a haven. She was comfortable in a way she had never experienced, and, for the moment, love seemed easy.

She set up a drawing board like the one she had in New York, near the window overlooking rue de La Chappelle with its restaurants. Here, in Paris, the moist air that drifted up to her through the open window smelled of Provence with garlic and basil and hot oil.

She sketched and painted in the mornings. Her paintings hung on the walls. She shopped in the neighborhood stores of the *quartier*, buying fresh chicken and newly baked bread, and *paté de campagne* from the *charcuterie*. The wine shop was right next door. She became a cook for the first time in her life, experimenting with herbs and fruit *tartes*.

They had a favorite bistro on a side street nearby. It was called *Le Petit Zinc*. Denys explained to her that most of the old bars were made of zinc, easy to clean the spilled wine, but many of them had been melted down by the Nazis during World War II for arms. Occasionally, he would take her to *Le Jazz Hot*, a small place on La Place de La Bastille where a trio supplied textured American jazz between the black enamel walls and swinging overhead lamps with lots of fringe. It was a small room, with a wonderful piano man, a *devotée* of Count Basie. The clop, clop of Sara's heels on the cobbled streets going home reminded her of the horses' sounds recorded in the courtyard of the stables of Vaux-Le-Vicomte, that day right before her father died.

She wasn't conscious of time. She was absorbed in living. One blustery, January night, Denys returned home, tired and a bit evasive. Sara poured him a glass of wine and busied herself with preparing the custard for a *crème caramel,* while he read the paper in the living room. When she peeked out to check on him, she saw he was studying the front page of <u>Le Monde</u>, which was spread out before him on the coffee table in front of the couch. His elbows were on his knees, fists under his chin as he pored over a picture and its adjacent article. He looked up to see her standing there.

"Come here, *chérie*," he said.

Sara sat beside him on the couch. He pointed to the picture in the newspaper.

It was the body of a man in a business suit, lying across a curb next to a parked Peugeot. The man had cropped hair and lay with one shoe off with his head on the pavement. The shoeless foot stretched into the gutter, the pale sock turning dark with blood.

She recoiled. She looked again, hard.

"It's Cutter." Then again, "Cutter!"

"Yes. Cutter."

"And his socks. He wore yellow socks, at the interview and at the Memorial Service. See there. See how pale they are?" She pointed to his feet in the picture. "This yellow sock is turning black with blood, it looks like. And see there's the big signet ring. He wore it both times I saw him."

Denys reached for both her hands. "I firmly believe he, too, was killed by The Company. 'Course I can't prove it."

"What? Not The Company!"

"Cutter couldn't control your father. Saul Mammon was giving information to both sides, some of it false, so he had to have your father 'taken out' and because of the publicity, including my own..." Denys Déols swallowed hard. "Cutter had to be 'taken out' himself."

"Couldn't they have just fired him?"

Denys laughed harshly. "He was in too deep. Cutter had to eliminate your father to protect himself. Maybe his superiors thought Saul Mammon had compromised him too, that he, Cutter, might have sold information for some of that glistening gold. Here, look," he said to Sara. "There's the gun, lying right beside Cutter's body. See? It says here in the article." He pointed to the line. "The killer must have thrown it there, wiped it clean."

"But I made him up, that cat killer. He's a product of my imagination."

"Oh he exists all right, maybe not with the glittering eyes you pictured." He smiled at her. "But believe me, he exists."

She was in shock. "What makes you think it was him? Did they catch him?"

He shook his head. "Do you know who the gun was registered to?"

"Oh no..."

"Your father."

"My God. The one in the suitcase..." Sara buried her face in her hands. "Not one death, now two."

Denys appeared rueful. "The pressure I brought on your father. The pressure I brought on Cutter." He took out his notebook and fumbled with it. "The story we're putting out, because it's the official line...it was...wait, I've got it here. 'Assassination in front of the American Embassy. U.S. Decoding expert shot down on the street,' he said, reading from the page. "Decoding expert?" He whacked his head in disgust.

"That gun," she said almost inaudibly.

"It's just a theory, of course, but I believe the hit man was ordered by Cutter to kill Saul Mammon. When he did it – Bulgarian

Method – he saw the gun in your father's suitcase and he took it. A touch of humor? Then came the publicity that threatened the cover-up, raised the cry of murder. Someone high up had to order the killer to take out Cutter. I really believe that's the way it happened."

"I thought the CIA didn't allow assassination," Sara said. She felt almost in a trance. "Is that just another big myth?"

"They don't assassinate outsiders, supposedly – even dangerous ones, but, among their own? It happens. The Intelligence bureaus are so compartmentalized. No one knows who's doing what to whom. And the killer used your father's gun, leaving it on the scene." Denys bowed his head. "Cutter couldn't handle Saul in the first place. Who could? But my articles really did it."

"Maybe early on, they were part of it, when they first came out, but its been months."

Sara was so disheartened she curled her knees under her on the couch, her body in a ball. She was haunted by a waking dream of a little boy in the window, standing there, looking out with wistful longing at the game he couldn't play, vulnerable to the sound of laughing voices in easy competition, unable to join in the fun. This separation had made him quite mad.

Combined with whatever twists and genetic oddities, Saul Mammon, née Mamminski, had grown up with a psychosis that at 60, had caused a creeper in the night, instrument of Government, to cause his death, and in perpetration, the death of that instrument as well. Finally, she realized she didn't care a whit who killed her father. He was gone. That's what mattered. That alone.

"What's it all about?" she managed to say, "the whole thing. What's the point?"

"You are, " Denys said with a smile. He moved close to her on the couch and put his arms around her. "You. Somehow your father's death gave new value to yourself. And you have me, you know. Is it enough?"

"I don't know."

He sat back lighting a cigarette, puffing away as he did, smoke rising in arcs to the ceiling.

"Think of the positives he left you - the two sides of the same golden coin. You're strong, yet you're weak enough to love." He grinned at her. "You're the juggernaut Mammon, yet you're gentle as a kitten. You're a painter and a cook and most of all, you're Sara. And your father?" he said thoughtfully. "He was the rogue elephant, the renegade bull roaring out of the bushes."

"DamnDéols," she said, rousing up. "How <u>do</u> you eat an elephant?"

"You don't."

LEGACY

n Denys' apartment, Sara was deep in a struggle to capture Saul Mammon's face. Once again. With dark charcoal lines, she aggressively pressed the cream-colored paper, as she examined her father's life. Power plays were his modus operandi: he used banks, getting them in so deep there was no way to refuse him more: he used people like Ephraim and Manny, the Terrible Twins, each a singular weapon, Ephraim because he was malleable, Manny because he was not; and she, his daughter, had felt his manipulation as he planned to offer her as a sop to de Bouchère in order to deliver up to himself the hotels of the Mediterranean.

As her fingers moved back and forth, she realized the biggest power play of all for the Man of History, she had always known as Daddy, was his exploitation of the Cold War, attempting to open the USSR to capitalism single-handedly. He was a solo act, never admitting that Armand Hammer or James Chapin or Herman Tyson of Petroleum Products had anything to do with his success. To unlock that new territory, to be first, Saul Mammon was not above passing secrets from the KGB to the CIA and vice versa. He worked both sides of the street.

He claimed that communism, not capitalism or democracy, was the communists' worst enemy and would in the end bring it down upon itself, and who better to know that, than Saul Mammon. He had started working at <u>The Daily Worker</u> during his Fuller Brush Man period, with elevator shoe propping open the potential buyer's door. He always said the Communist Party was a great way to meet people.

Denys Déols, through all of this, had become secondary to Sara, somehow in the background. Sara was still possessed by the image of Saul Mammon, and as she sat at her drawing board in the little salon of the apartment on rue de La Chapelle, sketching that face and examining Saul Mammon's flamboyant world, her father seemed to come alive. The drawing looked about to speak. The arched eagle-like brows, the deep-set eyes, drawn with dark-rimmed glasses on, giving the face definition, and the grin, veering to the left toward the deaf ear, the fine white teeth, the dimple, the cleft in the chin, they were all there.

There came the moment she could add nothing more.

Saul Mammon had always quoted the question, 'How do you eat an elephant?' And the answer he would give, 'bite by bite.' That's the way he lived.

In sudden discovery, Sara found herself murmuring out loud, "Maybe I should give it a try! Why not?"

Why not indeed!

Bite number one: Michelson Frères! Maybe the biggest bite of all.

Early that January morning, after speaking with Manny Kiser in New York City on the phone, she called the offices of Michelson Frères on Avenue Kléber. Manny, who had been wakened in the middle of the night, (the time in New York City being hours earlier) though hardly cordial, told her that to contact Michelson Frères might not be a bad idea.

"What you got to lose, kiddie?" were his last words to her as he hung up.

Sara spoke with André Michelson's secretary, explaining who she was and setting up an appointment with the boss for four o'clock that afternoon.

It was almost as if they were waiting for her.

Saul Mammon had been one of Micheleson Frères most feared and lucre-producing clients. The firm had been holding his financial share of franchise deals, including cases of the commemorative gold coins, already minted, slated for sale at the 1980 XXII Olympiad in Moscow the following summer.

Sara's appearance before the dapper, long nosed, André Michelson was like an apparition, a rather stunning version of Saul Mammon, which he as a Frenchman, fully appreciated. She seemed to him classy and intelligent, nobody's fool. The canny moneyman recognized the Mammon presence.

Sara requested an accounting of her father's holding as his legal heir, (of which there was no doubt) and, although Saul Mammon died intestate, he had been a full partner with the firm on the Olympic deals. With the help of the Michelson lawyers, and another call to Manny Kiser from Michelson's office, Sara came into a substantial sum, which included cash in exchange for the gold commemorative medallions, and some proceeds from the franchise earnings.

André Michelson felt shrewd because he knew how much more valuable the gold coin sets would become during and after the Olympics. The business with Sara went quickly because she didn't argue, and he was eager to be rid of Mammon obligations and association in view of the odor surrounding his death. In the French newspapers, when Saul Mammon was mentioned, his death was labeled a possible homicide.

Little did André Michelson know, at that time, that within weeks after this transaction, US President Carter would order the American boycott of the Moscow Olympic Games because of the Russian invasion of Afghanistan. André Michelson held medallions worth only their gold value, virtually nothing in his eyes, compared to what their potential had been. And Saul Mammon's franchise deals would be effectively negated by this Presidential move. André Michelson felt not so shrewd after all. In fact, he was in a fury at Sara Mammon's 'sleight of hand,' which seemed to have reached through the Iron Curtain and plucked money from the situation.

Typique!, André Michelson thought, inspecting his polished finger nails. One could expect no less of a Mammon! André had not seen the curtain closing in time, he admitted to himself with great chagrin. The Soviets never saw a dime. The American franchise companies saw no money at all, and Sara turned out not to be a poor girl after all.

She was Saul Mammon's daughter all right. With her coup, she felt it for the first time. She sensed her 'Saul' elements rising, but she determined to be different from him, without the quirks, without the deviousness. He never could go in a straight line. It had to be circuitous, she thought, envisioning that little boy from Brooklyn with the deaf ear, the soaring imagination, and the uneven gait.

Sara, with her new sense of strength, recognized another dilemma that had to be addressed. She realized that Denys and she had been through too much. His love had set her free to not be just Mammon's child, but to be herself, and, somehow, with the completion of her father's picture, with the absence of Saul to grapple with together, Denys was completed too.

They had grown more and more detached. The struggle over Saul was finished, and Denys seemed to her merely a French journalist devoted to his tasks. With all the affection, the "easy" love, Denys had now turned inward. He was growing distant. She began to notice he didn't even gesticulate as much.

She looked at her father's portrait. He seemed to whisper to her. "Time to move along, kid," and she knew it was so.

One lyrically beautiful, early spring evening, Denys came into the apartment later than usual. His face looked pale. Sara sat at her drawing board working on a view from the window. There was silence between them. She rose and moved to the bar table and poured two glasses of wine. "Would you like some?" she said raising the second glass to him.

"No. Not now."

"Perhaps you'd better." Her voice was soft.

"All right."

She handed him a glass and sat at the far end of the couch. He stood before her.

"Denys, it's getting to be time," she said quietly, after a long pause, regarding him somberly.

"Time for what?"

"For me to go home."

"I expected." He turned from her.

"But I'll see you again. I'll be back in Paris."

"Paris. *Bien sûr*. And you will see me if you wish. You know where I live." He began to pace the small room. "The only reason you didn't leave Paris before was because of the tapes, Cutter, the whole bloody mess."

"Not true. I stayed because of you."

"You stayed for your father's mystery, nothing else."

"No, Denys. It was you who were possessed by the mysteries, remember?"

"It's funny. Now you're never interested in my articles anymore. I told you I'm dogged about the truth. But other than your father's story, which was a battle-royal, in and out of bed," he added wryly, "you have never shown the slightest interest in my work. It's not necessary to be involved, but, *Mon Dieu,* you barely listen to me anymore, and you resent when work takes me away from you."

"Oh, my dear. You mean I have really swept you away with the rest of the debris?" she said ruefully.

"Yes," he grunted. "You were obsessed with Saul and since you've resolved some of the mystery and your own feelings about the murder..."

"The tragedy."

"Yes. It was that for you, especially since you had just begun to discover who each of you was. That was cut off, like a knife severing something alive. I understand that. But it's as if you have grown through me and come out the other side. I feel sometimes like a husk."

"Like I used you?" she said with a cry.

"In a way. I provided you with something to grapple. You were seeking your father and through his death you have found him. You don't need me anymore."

"Oh, Denys…I will never forget your role in unraveling…I'm so grateful."

"Gratitude," he snorted. "I don't want gratitude." There was a long pause. "You know something Sara? You have never even *thought* of drawing a picture of me," he said slowly.

She was nonplussed. It had never once occurred to her.

Déols shook his head sadly, and walked into the bedroom, as tears slowly rolled down her cheeks,

Sara slept fitfully on the couch. There had been nothing left between them, for some time it seemed, except for occasional sensual pleasure, and that just wasn't enough.

The following morning, she carefully packaged Saul's drawing and sent it to her mother. She knew it belonged to Anna.

"You don't know what this means to me," her mother said emotionally on the phone a few days later.

"Perhaps I do," said Sara. "I hoped maybe – well, maybe you'd understand him better."

"I thought I knew Saul. But I didn't. This picture captures him absolutely. The charms of 'Pecks Bad Boy.' Sara, it's astonishing. You caught him. I never thought it possible." Anna's voice quavered.

Sara felt her heart swell. "Do you remember when you claimed that there was a hollow in the center of my father's personality, a vacuum?"

"Yes, I remember."

"I don't see it that way, that there was nothing. There was something excruciatingly sensitive in that center core. Tender. Fearful. So afraid of being rejected by people."

Anna was silent. The airwaves crackled.

"Mama?"

"Yes."

"Especially by you, rejected by you."

Anna was silent, then, "We see him differently, darling," she said with a sigh.

"I know."

"I was his wife — on a par in terms of age and intellect, not so brilliant, of course, and he and I, we shared certain dreams. An offspring would see him, or me, from a different perspective than a mate. You know marriage is still the battle of the sexes, Sara, and with Saul there were such shocks and disappointments, things you couldn't possibly understand. But I know I disappointed him too," Anna said sadly. "It was bitter in the end, and I was scared out of my wits."

"I'm sure."

"But you, Sara. I know how hard this has been for you, what you have gone through."

"It's all right really. I'm all right."

"There was a moment before they both spoke at once. "I miss you," Anna said. "And I miss you," Sara whispered. She hung up.

She sat in the little window overlooking rue de La Chapelle. She had been drifting along living with Denys with little purpose except perhaps the simplicity of it. Now, *la vie bohème* was over. It was time to shed the fantasy, and prepare to fly.

Sara had kept the studio in Greenwich Village, subletting it, by the month, to an elderly art teacher. Now she wondered no more why she'd held on to it. It was a home. Paris with all its charms was not. The portrait of Saul was decisive for her. Her mother had confirmed it was truly he, and this brought Sara a powerful desire to embrace her life. She recognized her need, as Ephraim Bachman had felt the call of Israel.

"Like you, Ephraim," she murmured, "I'm a better woman than yesterday."

———

Two years later, Sara returned to Paris with a legal document arranged through Manny Kiser, releasing Saul's body to her alone. She determined to have him interred at Père Lachaise.

She did not call Denys.

She contacted an elderly Rabbi in the Marais district ready to perform the rituals necessary for a proper Jewish burial. On the morning of the interment, a shaken religious stood before Saul's headstone, alone with Saul's daughter.

"I have something to confess," he said, his voice troubled. "I was supposed to preside at his Memorial Service at the Coeur d'Or, two years ago."

"Oh?"

"I couldn't." The Rabbi blew his nose with a large handkerchief. "The night before, I wrestled with Saul Mammon's spirit until dawn. Never have I experienced this. Never. How he hated to give up. I was so conflicted, exhausted… I just couldn't face…" The Rabbi paused. "I let a young colleague take my place that day."

Sara and the elderly Rabbi stood before the grave, heads bowed.

"Peace, Daddy," she prayed.

The sky above Père Lachaise darkened. At the top of the hill of the ancient cemetery where they knelt, the wind quickened. Thunder crackled briefly, and rain began to fall, hard at first, gradually softening as the two hurried down to the street.

But for his small tomb, Saul Mammon's only legacy other than herself, was The Red Moon Hotel in Moscow, born in turmoil by merged monies, merged workers, merged goals, Sara thought, as she moved quickly in the rain beside the old man; The Red Moon, a remarkable achievement in a world where the Berlin Wall had stood and the Iron Curtain hung cold and intractable between nations.

"He'd rather be there in a suite, than here on a hill in the rain," she thought with a rueful smile.

The following day, as she was flying back to New York City from Paris, she seemed to hear the sound of her father's laughter as somewhere, high above the Concorde and the clouds and the firmament, he sat in some celestial corporate meeting – or incorporate meeting.

'It's fine, Sara. It's just fine up here, kid. For the first time, even I am not frightened by the view.'

And suddenly, neither was she.

POSTSCRIPT

R ipples emanating from Saul Mammon's life were cruel ones: the death of the CIA agent, for one; the demise of one of Saul's younger lawyers, who leapt to his death from the window in a law office building in Washington, DC, one week after Saul's murder (he had been instrumental in setting up dummy companies for his boss); and some years later, the beating of another lawyer, who was in Paris trying to track the remnants of Saul Mammon's European holdings. It happened in front of the Crillon Hotel, and that poor fellow spent six weeks in the American Hospital in that capital, being treated for his injuries. On his return to the United States, he quit the practice of law for good!

Coincidence? Serendipity? Or, just a simple twist of fate?

CPSIA information can be obtained
at www.ICGtesting.com
Printed in the USA
BVHW070105040220
571319BV00004B/16/J